All Endings Lead to New Beginnings

Medallion Mania

Prema Raghavan

notionpress.com

INDIA • SINGAPORE • MALAYSIA

ISBN 979-8-89233-871-4

This book is dedicated to all the lovely people who have thronged through my life and classrooms teaching me more than they will ever know.

Contents

Preface

The title of this novel, originally, was *The Knot of Hercules*. On a visit to Greece, I happened upon jewellery, in a museum shaped in a knot. I was intrigued to find it called *The Knot of Hercules* as it resembled the pattern on my ring. The ring, I wore, is known as the 'pavitra mothiram' in Kerala, and the design symbolises the knot tied to Darba grass when performing religious rituals. Finding jewellery which incorporated the knot in Greece made me wonder about its origin.

The use of various types of amulets and protective elements in the form of jewellery is well known. The caduceus symbol is used, even in modern times, as a talisman. On the wings of imagination, it has entered the narrative replacing *The Knot of Hercules.*

I must confess that my characters often refuse to toe the line proposed by me. They take on lives of their own and insist on telling their own stories. Radha for instance made me rewrite her diary. She accused me of not relating her experiences in enough detail.

All the places which form the locale of this novel are intimately known to me. Kodungallur is the place from which my parents hail. The legends and tales with which this novel is peppered are ones I grew up hearing. Kodungallur is believed to have been the ancient port city of Muziris, and the gateway through which traders and people of various religions and ethnicity entered the country. For me, it is a land which is stamped on my mind and imprinted in my genes. To write about it was an act of discovering impressions buried deep within my psyche. The attic where Nina discovers palm leaf manuscripts existed in our old, ancestral home. As a child, I was fascinated by its dusty interiors filled with memorabilia. However, we were warned to stay away since it was also the haunt of civet cats. The attic for me had all the fascination of a forbidden space and therefore has found its way into my novel.

I have not tied up all the loose ends in a neat bow. Life is about an ongoing process. It refuses to be contained within the lifetime of an individual, and we do not witness the endings of beginnings. So, read on and make your own conclusions from what the eyes see and the mind creates.

PART - 1

What we call the beginning is often the end

And to make and end is to make a beginning.

The end is where we start from. And every phrase

And sentence that is right (where every word is at home,

Taking its place to support the others,

The word neither diffident nor ostentatious,

An easy commerce of the old and the new,

The common word exact without vulgarity,

The formal word precise but not pedantic,

The complete consort dancing together)

Every phrase and every sentence is an end and a
beginning,

Every poem an epitaph.

—T.S. Eliot, from "Little Gidding",
Four Quartets.

Chapter I

The Apple Orchard

There are some paths which lead you back to where it all began. Nina did not know she was on one of them as she opened the Google map on her phone. The battery was rapidly dwindling, and the sky lowered with the approach of darkness, descending like a sheath to blot out the landscape. They had passed Shimla an hour ago, veering onto a narrow mountain road. She had tried desperately to get directions from the resort manager who calmly told her to trust Google, and they would arrive eventually. Derek was sitting forward, eagerly scanning the horizon for some large geese which had flown past signalling a water body nearby. He drove instinctively, anticipating every turn on the mountainous terrain. Nina turned away with a sigh. With excitement, she noted that they were passing an apple orchard. The ripening apples were encased in a large net to protect them from hail and vermin. It reminded her of the net, she placed over rollers, after setting hair. They had to be close; they had entered a vast sea of fruit, and she smelt its rich, heavy scent as she drew the car windows down. The voice on Google told her that in 350 meters, their location would be to the left. Scarcely believing, she strained her eyes to catch a sign. There was none, but

Derek with the honed instincts of the much-travelled drove up beside rough, granite slabs which descended into the midst of long, colonial-style buildings.

Nina and Derek were on a delayed vacation; Nina refused to call it a honeymoon since it was four years since they were married. Nina, an aesthetician, had met Derek at the housewarming party of a friend. He was the last of the Anglo-Indians to stay back, refusing to migrate to Australia with the rest of his generation. He was a naturalist and the Director of the Centre for Rural Technology. It was his passion for all things which grew and flew which had brought them together. Nina found her job as an aesthetician, deeply satisfying; she worked at enhancing and restoring the natural beauty of the human form. Derek was a messiah and lover of all that grew in nature. They had drifted easily into a relationship and then subsequently into marriage. Nina was a Hindu by birth, but belonging to different faiths had not dissuaded them. Nina's permissive parents and the absence of Derek's, now settled in Australia, had made it easy for them to register their marriage on a suitable day and in Nina's words, "carry on as usual". Their romance would not have been a Netflix blockbuster. There were no opposing forces to carry the story beyond the first couple of episodes. Fairy tale endings do not hold the attention of even wide-eyed children who were yet to lose their milk teeth.

Nina got out of the car. Stretching up, she stood on her toes to ease the tension along her back. In the gathering gloom, she could see rough-hewn granite steps that descended into the darkness below. There were, however, no handrails alongside the stairway into the unknown. She was about to give vent to her dismay, when a head appeared over the top of the steps, followed by another. Their baggage was plucked out of their hands and embraced by the smiles and welcoming gestures of the striking-looking duo, who appeared to be cloned, they began their descent. Derek bounded ahead; Nina followed pausing frequently, all too aware of the perils of descending without support.

Their suite was all glass, and Nina drew back the curtains so that she could look at the splendour of a sky ablaze with stars; the constellations seemed so close, that she thought she could reach out and hold them in her palm. The shield of Saturn, and the archer representing Sagittarius were discernable to her practised eye. Sighing, she turned away. The murky skies of the city, in which she lived, had all but obliterated her childhood passion for stargazing. Derek was asleep, on his back, one arm shielding his eyes. She eased him onto his side, a trick she had learnt to stop him from snoring. Marital wisdom, she thought. Too tired to go through her elaborate, nightly skin routine, she slid quickly under the sheets, breathing in their clean, washed smell and the next she knew was the sound of the clink of a spoon on a teacup. The sky outside their window was crimson streaked with gold. Dawn was just breaking, and for a while, she lay studying the sky. Venus would be a morning star at this time of the year. She squinted into the morning light, trying to spot it. Derek came around to pull the quilt off her, his eyes teasing. He held her, warm and still half asleep, and she snuggled closer in response. As he bent to kiss the soft hollow of her throat, the phone rang, loud and demanding; the harshness grating their roused senses. It was a reminder from the reception; breakfast in forty-five minutes before the morning trek.

Nina rolled over and bounded off with a half-laugh. The magic was still there. Of Irish ancestry, Derek's eyes were hazel with green flecks, which turned dark with the passion of making love or in a fight. The first couple of years had seen them stalk around each other and stalk away. Now, they knew when to hold their peace. Arguments, hardly, if ever, precipitated into the fierce bloody battles which had drawn blood. To do him justice mused Nina, he fought fair. But, the more he tried to quash an argument with logic, the louder she grew. She would remember with startlingly, vivid detail, every slight she had encountered in their relationship. He would barricade himself and retreat into a silence which could last for days unless she broke in and coaxed him back, and then it was as if nothing had happened. Nina was an only child, and seeking attention was a wired-in instinct. Derek's total absorption with his numerous environmental concerns was often the bone of contention. Nina had learnt to reconcile with the fact that Derek was a man of multiple interests. He was a well-known columnist and a photographer. His research articles and efforts in conserving local flora and fauna had won global acclaim.

The trek had sounded exciting, and the presence of the elderly Israeli couple who had joined had given Nina a false sense of complacency. As it turned out, they were seasoned trekkers and could navigate the course easily. Nina focused on not skidding on the pebbles and boulders strewn across the path. Sometimes, the path narrowed as it met meandering streams. Here, a trekker had to leap across, moving from one boulder to the next. She could hear bird calls, and a few laughing thrushes accompanied them, chuckling merrily. They were not a welcoming party as Nina would romantically have assumed earlier but for the knowledge gained from living with the 'Birdman', a name she had coined for Derek. Here as elsewhere, nature forged a symbiotic relationship. Their feet had sent insects scuttling out of hiding, and the birds had come to feed on them. Derek was deep in conversation with their guide, his attention held by the presence of the unusual flora which grew at these heights. The Israeli man, introduced as Ben, lifted Nina and guided her over the last, narrow stretch of boulders which looked as if they would go rolling, carrying the intrepid trekker down the chasm on either side. His wife Rachel, tall and strapping, jumped over the boulders like a mountain goat.

The trek ended in a church, perched high, on the craggy hill. It was the church of St Mary, a brightly painted, pretty wooden building with magnificent stained-glass windows. Built in the nineteenth century, the church figured in the story, *Lispeth*, by Rudyard Kipling which Nina had read and now she gazed at it trying to recognise features from the story. There was a little garden which skirted the front of the church, and it was abloom with begonias, petunias, flocks, dahlias and some other plants that she did not know the names of. While their guide led the others to the small graveyard which lay behind the church, Nina sat, her eyes closed, sniffing the bouquet of fragrance in the warm air. It had grown warm. She felt the trickle of sweat gather around the waistband and where her hat sat on her forehead. She shrugged off her jacket, pulling out the chain from under her T-shirt. Having freed the pendant from the hollow between her breasts, she wiped it gently with her hanky and was about to tuck it back when she heard a loud gasp.

"Isn't that the caduceus?", asked Rachel as she bent forward, her expression a mixture of incredulity and awe.

The pendant was a medallion in the shape of two snakes, their bodies intertwined in a knot around a rod. On top of the rod were two wings. The heads of the snakes were facing each other. It was made of gold studded with topaz, ruby and emerald. The snakes held between their raised hoods, a sapphire, the size of a pea. The mid-day sun fell on the brightly coloured gems, and for a moment the snakes seemed to move in the blaze of iridescent light. Rachel moved back, her expression changing to one of recognition.

She looked at Nina as if seeing her for the first time as she asked the question, "Where did you get that?"

"What do you mean? Get that? Get what?"

"I should have phrased it differently. Didn't mean to offend you. It's just that…," she trailed off.

"This pendant is my mother's and has been in our family for generations," replied Nina.

"Is there something the matter? You look startled," Nina wanted to know. She was feeling flustered by the strangeness of Rachel's continued scrutiny.

Rachel who was still studying the medallion, strung on a delicate rope chain, looked up as if to reply. Breaking the intensity of her gaze, she smiled confidingly at Nina. She lowered herself on the wooden, garden bench and turning to Nina said, "Your jewellery is the replica of our family insignia. We are Jews of European descent, and this particular design is very distinctive. I was startled to see it on you."

Nina slipped the chain off her neck and held it out to Rachel who inspected it closely.

Tracing the pattern gently with her finger Rachel said, "This centerpiece is the caduceus. It is the staff you find in representations of the Greek god, Hermes. According to Greek mythology, Hermes was the son of Zeus, the king of Greek gods."

She paused to gather her thoughts, squinting at the fierce noon sun. "Hermes was a precocious child and even as an infant in the cradle had a sharp mind and a keen sense of humour. The tricks he played were amusing rather than malicious. Perhaps, I am being partial. I do have an enduring fondness for him." She paused and turned to Nina, her dark eyes brimming with amusement.

"According to legend, Hermes stole a herd of sacred cows from his brother, Apollo, soon after being born. Apollo knew who the culprit was and was furious."

"My mother would love to hear the story behind what she regards as mere jewellery," said Nina.

With a smile, Rachel continued her narration. "When Apollo stormed in, Hermes pretended innocence. He lay fast asleep, a little baby in the cradle, the very picture of innocence. Maia, his mother, was not fooled and his father merely chuckled. Poor Apollo. Hermes wanted to placate his brother so he created a lyre out of a hollowed tortoiseshell. He was a clever trickster, but charming. Zeus loved him, and Apollo soon became his greatest friend and protector. It is Apollo who gave Hermes this golden staff. He had a way of winning over his foes," Rachel broke off.

"Go on," said Nina. She was intrigued. The pretty pattern on her pendant had significance. It indeed had one, beyond anything Nina could have ever imagined.

"Well," continued Rachel, her voice low and slightly breathy, "Hermes was the only god who could travel between the world of the living and the underworld of the dead. A captivating and not wholly moral god, he became the patron of thieves, gamblers, liars, travellers, traders and all those who inhabit the murky world of commerce. Our forefathers had their share of black sheep, but the majority were engaged in maritime trade along the silk route."

Holding out the medallion to light, where it seemed to glint at them, Rachel continued, "The caduceus became a mascot worn by travellers who sailed to unknown destinations to trade. Perhaps, that is how this reached India. The symbol was adapted slightly by my forefathers, making it unique. Notice, how the snakes are not merely coiled around the staff. The tails are tied in the knot of Hercules."

Nina gazed at the knot, which looked rather like the one on the ring she was wearing.

"Is this also a knot of Hercules?" Nina asked, displaying her ring.

"Yes, it is," said Rachel. "It is found in a lot of jewellery, particularly wedding rings, and has become a symbol of love and commitment. It is the pairing of the caduceus with the knot of Hercules which makes this piece, such a rare one."

"I wonder what the story is behind this lovely pendant? It is an original. Have you ever got it valued? Don't," Rachel added, "ever get it valued."

They could hear the sound of the men's voices approaching. Nina hastily slipped on the chain, tucking it out of sight, before shrugging on the jacket. The peace of the morning was broken by the harsh call of a lapwing which flew overhead. Nina looked at Rachel's hands, pale and spangled with age spots; they were large and calloused. She got up and moved a few paces away feeling oddly disturbed.

The guide, sent by the resort, had gone to track the car which would be taking them to Stokes Apple

Orchard. On the short drive to the orchard, Nina was quiet. Derek had chosen to sit with the driver leaving the seat beside her vacant. He had a child-like fascination for the new, an insatiable curiosity which was one of his most endearing qualities. But today, it made Nina feel forsaken and when they got off, she walked briskly to study the board outside the farm. Derek came to stand near her, and she moved a few paces away provoking a stare. She donned her glasses; they were huge and made her look fragile. The information on the board was a recognition of the contribution made by Stokes to the local community of his times, and his selfless efforts towards the progress of the country, he so willingly embraced.

This orchard like the other apple orchards in the Thanedar Kotgarh region owes its prosperity to Samuel Satyanand Stokes. (!882-1946). The entire region is indebted to this ingenuous missionary from Philadelphia who introduced them to apple farming. Samuel Stokes was so moved by the poverty of the people of Kotgarh that he determined to do his best to alleviate their suffering. Giving up all his worldly possessions, he lived in a cave. The Sahib became a Sadhu who studied Hindu philosophy and adopted the Gandhian way of life. He dressed in Khadi, married a local girl and in 1932 became a Hindu. He participated in India's struggle for freedom and was jailed along with other freedom fighters. It is said that when the Britishers saw this American dressed in a khaki coat, dhoti and cap spinning his charka every day, they almost had a fit.

They rambled through an orchard; the short, stocky branches were studded with fruit larger than any Nina had seen before. It had grown warm, and Nina could feel the perspiration bead her upper lip. The Israeli couple were ahead, deep in conversation, and Derek seemed to have disappeared into the gloom of the orchard. She crunched on an apple and felt the juice run down her chin onto her clothes. She slipped off her jacket and tied the sleeves around her waist, reaching up to pin her hair in place. Slackening her pace, she stopped to click the picture of a young woman gathering apples strewn under the trees. She was beautiful, with high cheekbones, sloe eyes and the ruddy complexion of the local women. The child she carried, seemed welded to her hips as she walked along balancing a full basket on her head. She smiled, looking full at Nina as she passed, her body moving with grace and rhythm. Coming close, she reached out to remove a bit of the fruit from Nina's hair which had come loose, cascading in dark rivulets from the bun into which she had gathered it. Her eyes reflected her appreciation, and for a moment the two stood gazing at each other in a primordial communion, antiquating any form of verbal expressions. The spell was broken by the sound of approaching footsteps as Derek emerged from a canopy of trees and hastened towards her. The woman moved away with a quick bob of her head, drawing her veil over her head.

In the shadowy half-light of the grove, the man approaching could have been young Stokes; Derek had the same intensity of gaze and fixity of purpose.

He walked towards her, his eyes intent on finding her. If she were ever lost in a desert thought Nina wryly, she would be certain of rescue. His eyes met hers and burrowed deep within and she surrendered as she had done, the very first time they met. Then, she had felt illuminated to be the focal point of his gaze, it never wavered in its attention Now, she knew better. He gazed at the universe with the same fervour; a man held in thrall by the mystery of the universe. She felt contrite. She had sulked all morning for being left on her own. Linking arms, they walked speaking of the man whose presence was still palpable nearly three-quarters of a century later.

Derek spoke with reverence about the man whose philanthropy had not received enough attention in the annals of history. Back then, apples grown were either berry apples or sour, cooking apples. The local farmers lived in penury and ignorance of new farming methods. Stokes brought back saplings of several different kinds of apples, one of which was the delicious, juicy red apples that Himachal Pradesh was famed for. With experimentation, he learnt that the climate of Himachal Pradesh with its long winters, adequate rainfall and rich, loamy soil was best suited to the Missouri variety of apples. He went, a messiah among people, with offers of free saplings. But the local people were averse to change. They looked upon him as an eccentric and feared anything which would disturb the steady rhythm of their lives. Even poverty can become a habit. They tore off the saplings which he planted. Finally, when they saw a few of the apples which had survived molestation, first a few and later other farmers switched to the new variety. Within a decade, trucks were transporting apples to every nook and cranny of India. All that it took one generation to grow wealthy on the riches of the soil was to replace the emptiness of routine with the potential of the unexplored.

The air around them was suffused with the aroma of puris bubbling in oil making Nina realise that she was famished. Breakfast had been a hurried meal, and the long, arduous walk had made her ravenously hungry. All her senses shut down. Derek's words faded into a distant hum, and she hastened forwards into a clearing where there stood a pergola swathed in a profusion of creepers, which flowered all the way across the roof, running down the sides in a splendid display of blooms. The Israeli couple sat on wicker chairs while their guide from the resort, Makhan, hovered around supervising arrangements for lunch. Nina flopped on a chair opposite them and shut her eyes, enjoying the respite from exertion.

"Beer madam," Madan stood over her with a pitcher overflowing with a frothy, amber fluid. "Apple cider," he corrected himself.

The others were already quaffing from large, glass mugs, and she could hear odd ends of their conversation.

She smiled her thanks as she reached out and lifted a glass of the golden cider, beaded with bubbles and garnished with a slice of fresh orange. She took one reviving sip and then another. Rachel was addressing her, her face crinkled in puzzlement. Nina realised she had not responded to Rachel's query.

"I was telling Derek that you must visit Israel soon and experience living in a Kibbutz."

"I think I must have dozed off for a bit. Do you live in one?"

"Yes, we do. Both Ben and I have lived in the same Kibbutz… perhaps all our lives… we returned to it after completing our military service."

Nina looked up with interest… no wonder her hands were so capable looking… they could well have been the hands of a farmer or an assassin. Hands spoke to Nina; tending them was her profession.

"Do women serve in combat zones? Can they gun down young children who are being recruited in armed conflicts?"

"Age and genders are blurred… you shoot to kill or risk dying."

Food had arrived and Makhan cleared his throat to indicate it was time to eat. Nina's eyes were caught by the beautiful colours on the ceramic pottery. They were the colours of a sunset and gleamed in the slanting rays which streamed in through the woven roof. She held a soup bowl in her hand, gently turning it over. Makhan approached her with the soup tureen and in response to her query said they were from Khurjah, near Delhi. Nina sighed. She would have to wait., something, she was not good at. In any case, they could not carry much. They would be flying out of Delhi to Paris in just 72 hours.

Derek was in deep conversation with a young man, a pahadi, who had been frying puris, just outside the gazebo. She could hear snatches of conversation. He was trying to locate the red-headed vulture, a rare sighting, only possible in these parts. Ben pulled up a chair to indicate that she should join them.

"No meat for you?"

"None… I am a happy vegetarian."

"Happy vegetarian?"

"I love all veggies and don't fancy eating anything which swims, flies or runs," said Nina with a grin. The carrot and pomegranate salad in hung curd was divine.

"Is this a religious practice or a conviction?" asked Rachel.

"I didn't eat any meat as a child… and later it became about not preying on creatures great and small."

"Are many Hindus vegetarian?"

'Not according to the last survey. Most Hindus don't eat beef though… a cow is a sacred animal."

"How about Derek?"

"Derek believes that humans are omnivores."

"Why else would they have canine teeth?" asked Derek, devouring the last bit of apple pie.

It was so unfair that he could eat a whole tableful and still not gain a gram. Nina glowered. She could have gladly accepted another piece of the flaky, cinnamon-sprinkled pie.

"Are you a Hindu too?"

With a name like Derek, wondered Nina.

"I am a baptized, non-practicing Christian."

There was an awkward silence which Nina broke with her favorite quip,

"You can never, ever be a non-practicing Hindu. You are born a Hindu and it stays that way."

Derek laughed, he ought to have known it was coming. Ben and Rachel exchanged amused glances.

"That is not entirely true, Nina. Hinduism is a way of life. How else did Stokes a Christian missionary become Satyanand, a Hindu?"

Rachel said, "Our son is vegan and against all forms of militarism. He will have to serve a prison sentence to be exempted."

"Perhaps not," interceded Ben. "His veganism will save him. He will be exempted for being a pacifist… someone with a conscience who abhors all forms of violence. He will be exempted on the grounds of his objection to war being moral, rather than political."

Nina had never been able to perceive how people could love their pets, be crusaders for wildlife and still consume what had been killed as food. Derek argued that predation was nature's instinctive response to preventing chaos and a deficit of resources. Predators created a healthy ecosystem, he insisted, by ensuring the survival of the fittest. Humans, he argued, were hunters and food gatherers. Eating meat was in congruity with the food chain, which if broken would lead to the death of many known species.

The sun was fading from the horizon and the shadows of the flowers danced along the floor.

Makhan came in to announce that the sales counter was open.

The apples were sorted out by size. Some of the large ones were melon-sized. Ben and Rachel exclaimed in dismay about not being able to carry them back home and stepped back to let the other couple order.

Nina pulled a face, "None for us either. This time, next week, we will be in Nice."

Rachel held out a hand, taking Nina's in hers.

"This meeting was not accidental."

Noticing Nina's startled expression, she added, "It was kismet as they call it in these parts which brought us together here. I feel like I am meeting my own kin."

Turning to include Derek, she added, "My niece and her husband have an organic vineyard near Nice. This is the season of harvesting grapes and making wine. Visit them… the experience will be authentic… not included in a tour book."

Derek was a wine aficionado and meeting people who created wine was the reason for their visit to the French Riveria. Being at a winery, taking notes, sampling the wine and speaking the language only wine lovers know, nothing could be better.

"Kismet indeed. Rachel. Speaking of wines, I didn't have to open a bottle for the genie to appear."

They drove back in silence. It was a day to remember, a memory-making day, and for each of them, there was something to capture and recall.

Nina fell into bed after a long soak in the tub, refusing to leave the comfort of the bed for dinner. Her legs felt leaden; something was hovering at the edge of her consciousness. She was too tired to dwell on it. Then she was drifting along with a current. It was a whirlpool and she was sinking. She screamed and woke up to Derek holding her and stroking her gently as if calming a child. She turned towards him, and the momentum of the strokes changed.

"Come here," she said pulling down his head.

His mouth fastened and held. She raised herself, her back arched and welded to him. Time stopped. Nothing existed except mouths and fingers and the chorus of sensations along the skin.

"Now," she rasped, her voice caught in her throat.

Outside in the sky through the glass windows, there were tiny, quick streaks of light, a meteor shower which erupted into blazing brightness. She shuddered, falling back as he sank into her. Then all grew still and calm.

Chapter II

The Vineyard

She was back again in the mausoleum. It was that hour
when day gathers up her skirt, holding it to a side, before
skipping over the horizon into the embrace of darkness.
The air was redolent with the smell of marigolds, the
fragrance wafting up in the still-warm air. Nina came
to the place often. It adjoined the apartment building
in which her parents lived. No one ever bothered her;
there was a feeling of unutterable peace. The tombs bore
inscriptions, some of which were nearly effaced by time.
She would pause to read and wonder what the lives of
those who were interred had been like as she walked
along the paths, carefully tended by the caretaker. It
had been a month since they had moved in, and though
no one was permitted to enter, Nina had found a way
to sneak in. She could easily straddle the little wicket
gate on the wall, separating the mausoleum from the
apartment building. No one had chased her away, so she
came on most afternoons, seeking the sense of freedom
which accompanied wide-open spaces. Sometimes, she
would bring a book and read for hours, undisturbed.
On one such day, the quiet of the drowsy afternoon
was shattered by a loud shriek, startling Nina from her
reverie. It came again and yet again, the sound of a soul

in agony. Nina screamed and ran blindly, tripping over a root. She scrambled up, turning to see if someone was pursuing her. At that precise moment, a peacock came strutting out and flew onto the branches of a tree giving forth the same raucous cries. When she reached home, her knees and palms bloodied, her mother demanded an explanation. The mausoleum became out of bounds. Young girls were not safe in lonely places, not even among the dead, declared her mother. She would hear that cry many times but always at a distance.

That morning, it broke through her slumber. The cries sounded nearby. How could there be a peacock in Nice? But the cry, she realised as she came wide awake, was different. It was loud and insistent, without the deep throbbing melancholia of a peacock's call. The balcony door was open, and she could smell the sea and hear the steady drum of its waves. She gathered up the coverlet and wrapped it around her shoulders like a shawl as she made for the balcony. The breeze which buffeted her tasted salty on her lips and stung her eyes. Facing her was a pier, with seagulls squawking and flying in circles around a familiar figure. Derek stood palms cupped and held out, his shoulders squared and his feet planted wide apart. The seagulls swooped in and carried off bits of something, which she could not discern from where she was watching. His head was raised as if to sniff the salty tang of the air. The birds ranged around him, emboldened by the firm, unwavering steadiness of his posture. He was like a magnet thought Nina. All manners of creatures gravitated towards him. Babies, puppies and those living with a mental illness moved towards him, unbidden. There was a sense of deep compassion which radiated like a wave, attracting the most vulnerable. She knew its pull; it had been an easy surrender.

She would have run down to be a part of the spectacle of man and bird that had begun to attract the attention of passers-by, but she needed to get dressed. They would be leaving in an hour for the vineyard. Rachel's cousin, Sharon, had been very persuasive over the phone, and while bikes were available for the adventurous, Sharon was coming to get them.

Nina chose a wide-necked plain top to go over a pair of palazzos and fixed the length of her chain with the medallion so that the knot of Hercules rested between her shoulder blades. It was on display; she was seeking some answers.

Sharon was waiting in the lobby and approached them the moment they came within sight. She was a small woman with a curly mop of short, dark hair which framed a face furrowed with wrinkles. Sun exposure, Nina thought; the aesthetician in her making a quick diagnosis of skin type and condition. Sun exposure without protective headgear or cream could lead to a wrinkled appearance. Moreover, European skin tended to be thinner and more fragile than Asian ones. Sharon's eyes met hers with a smile. They were a warm amber, and she seemed genuinely delighted to make their acquaintance. Along with a spontaneous conviviality which Nina guessed was a part of her personality, was an air of self-possession. She had come for them in a Land Rover; a sedan, Nina thought would have been more her style. She clambered in first, Derek choosing to sit in front. Sharon drove intuitively and well, all her movements fluid and composed. They passed through small villages, the squares blazing with pots of summer flowers suspended from hooks. Then, they were climbing a hill. The zig-zagging roads gave them a view of the shimmering, sunlit expanse of the turquoise blue sea on one side and splendid, wooded peaks on the other. It was a visual treat, and before they even knew it they had arrived at the vineyard. There was a burst of sporadic barking at a distance which was quickly hushed. Then a figure emerged, tall, bald and burly. He went straight to the driver's seat and lifted Sharon to the ground as if from a horse. Derek had got out already, and Nina followed. She nearly tumbled in her hurry, missing the last step. The chivalrous man was Peter, Sharon's husband and the owner of the vineyard. They were soon to discover that he was passionate about everything to do with the making of wine. This was a real dirt-under-your-fingernails farm as Peter made minimal use of machinery.

The harvesting of grapes was still in progress, and Peter lovingly took them on a trail of luscious grapes, which were both sweet and tart. He broke off several bunches for Nina to pop into her mouth. The tour ended at the winepress. Peter explained that after fermentation, the wine was placed in huge vats, and kept in the storehouse. The vats were made of different kinds of wood which added tertiary aromas to the wine due to prolonged contact. The primary notes could be fruity like pear, peach or apricot. From this, the wine aged in wooden vats or barrels, acquired aromas of cinnamon, hazelnut, toast, leather, vanilla or sweet spices; different aromas depending on the type of wood in which the ageing of wine took place. Fascinated, they took a sip from each of the vats trying to distinguish the bouquet of flavours, going from the sweeter, rounder wines to the more acidic ones.

Sharon had laid out lunch under the spreading branches of an old gnarled tree. Shrimp canapes and onion soup were served as starters. The main course was a choice of fried chicken and curried crab. To Nina's relief, there was some wild rice, potatoes, pasta and an array of steamed vegetables. Next came a selection of local cheese, and for dessert, there were crepes made of banana, rum and hazelnut. There was an assortment of wines to choose from with each course. This pairing of excellent food with gourmet wines was a gastronomical delight that had Nina in a swoon. She was afloat on the rays of sunlight that filtered through the leaves of the trees, floating like a balloon to merge with the blue of the sky. Derek was saying something to her, but she wanted to keep soaring. She drank thirstily from the goblet of golden wine, tasting notes of fruit and honey, shutting her eyes against a world that had turned dazzling bright. She would shut her eyes for just a moment. It was so peaceful… she could hear a flute playing at a distance… was it a lyre, perhaps? Sharon brought in the coffee… Nina drank it black. The evening shadows had lengthened, and a cool breeze had begun to blow. Would they like to see the villa? Sharon rose from her chair, and Nina followed her. The whole experience had a dream-like quality. The men had moved away in search of a skylark that was singing deep within the gloom of the adjoining woods.

The first impression Nina got was that the outside light had followed them indoors. There was a pervading sense of luminosity and brightness. There were more windows than walls, and floor-length paintings in radiant hues took up the remaining space. Nina sighed in ecstasy. She had not seen a more beautiful room, not even in the swanky homes she visited. Sharon smiled at her warmly and picking up a beautifully crocheted shawl, draped it around her.

"This is for you. I began it when Rachel sent a picture."

"How did you know that I would come?" asked Nina. Her dark eyes widened as she stared at Sharon.

"The medallion would bring you seeking answers. There is nothing magical. It just is."

"Meaning?"

"We all need to delve into mysteries. Unearthing the mystery of the universe is what humankind has been doing for aeons. All the voyages over the seas, space travel and even travelling back in time to discover our beginnings is a compulsive need. If you were not a seeker, the medallion would not have revealed itself to you. Meeting Rachel was no accident."

"You mean, Rachel followed me to Thanedar?"

"That was a chance encounter." She paused to look Nina full in the face.

"It is called serendipity. You have opened yourself up to your life changing, or moving in a new direction by being somewhere, or doing something you wouldn't normally."

That is bang on, thought Nina. She was not the adventurous sort. The trek had sent her adrenalin soaring. Was this the outcome?

"Rachel piqued my curiosity. But we might never have met if Nice hadn't been on our itinerary."

"You would have met someone else. Serendipity expresses itself in everyday events, in chance meetings with people or discoveries which bring unexpected life changes."

Sharon pulled up her top to reveal a waist chain with a clasp which was the replica of the one worn by Nina. Unclasping it, she held it up for Nina to see." This is probably of a later date than yours. Look, the gems in your medallion are larger. The sapphire must date back to the time of the pharaohs."

"Is this a symbol of clanship? Am I missing something? It was never mentioned by anyone. No one in the family. My mom, who finds all the jewellery she has mere clutter, never wore it."

"Kinship is the word I would choose if I had to use a word to describe this bond. It has existed for centuries. Our people recognize their kind through the knot of Hercules uniting the tails of the snakes on the caduceus. They look out for each other. The power lies in the mantle of protection it wraps the wearer in."

"How on earth was this not known to any one of us? I know it has been passed over generations to the firstborn. I don't know when the tradition began. Perhaps, there is something in that. I always thought it was a family heirloom, too beautiful to rest in a bank locker."

"True… it's an exquisite piece. It would be a pity to bury it in a vault!" exclaimed Sharon.

She paused. Her expression turning sombre she added, "The symbol has been stolen and used for ill-gotten gains. It is better to keep it hidden, at least while you are in Europe… unless you need help. Then it is like an SOS. A code to signal distress. Help will come, sometimes in most unexpected ways."

Derek entered and paused momentarily. He looked at Nina, taking in her flustered appearance.

"Are you alright?" his expression asked before he turned to Sharon.

"Peter is taking me to the cellar to pick some wine. Only two bottles, I am afraid. Not permitted to carry back more. Do help us choose."

There was an iron spiral staircase leading down to a dark cellar. As she followed in their wake, Nina choked back a giggle. Life had suddenly thrown the game of snakes and ladders at her, she reflected. Derek turned and raised his eyebrows. He watched her descend before moving to join Peter. She would not tell him yet. She had to figure it out for herself first.

The drive back home was silent. Sharon had excused herself on the grounds that she had to feed her cats. As dusk gathered, feline shapes began to dot the landscape. These ranged from kittens to middle-aged tabbies.

"These have been abandoned by their owners and would die of starvation if I did not feed them. Some disappear over time, but most return daily... just before darkness descends. Cats are mysterious creatures. Who knows where they go?" wondered Sharon with a shrug.

The drive home was silent. Peter played music from a local station, while Nina snuggled against Derek. There would be time to think it over. Too much was happening and all too suddenly. For now, Nina decided to push it to the back of her mind and enjoy each exquisite day, which came clad in the blue and gold of summer days, along the Mediterranean coast.

They had a whole week left of revelling in the most beautiful of all cities in Riveria, Nice.

Nice was like a painting by the impressionists with dramatic highlights and shadows. The ever-changing colours of the Mediterranean landscape were visible from the Promenade des Anglais where Derek and Nina spent every morning of their week-long stay in Nice. The azure blue of the sea would change to cobalt under the summer sun, and the evening sky would arrive flushed in shades of pink and orange-hued clouds. On clear days the sun would sink like the fiery ball of Monet's painting. The promenade was an emblem of Nice, and there were strollers, cyclists and some skaters at all times of the day. Palm trees flanked the legendary street along which were formal, stylised gardens. Giant yachts could be seen out in the beautiful sea. Nice, the throbbing centre of the French Riveria was the playground of the wealthy and the epicureans. They watched fascinated a man feeding honey- water to hummingbirds from a feeder. Derek was unhappy with the idea of a handheld device. Birds would lose their natural fear of humankind, and with the loss of that survival instinct would come captivity. To Nina's relief, the man was out of calling distance, and she quickly diverted Derek's attention to a group of young men playing beach football.

On the last day, they went to the Musée d'Art Moderne et d'Art Contemporain. The museum had a representation from the 1960s and 1970s, including pop art and American abstract art. Later, they walked to Place Massena Square. It was a beautiful plaza which lay at the end of the old town, near the new shopping arcade. The flooring was a geometric black-and-white design which glistened when the square was lit in the evening. That was that moment when the strange sculptures at the end of posts along the square suddenly came alive in pulsating colours, and applause resounded across the square.

After posing in front of the fountain adorned with a sculpture of Poseidon, Nina was ready to engage in her favourite sport, people-watching. The square had many charming sidewalk cafes, bakeries, and restaurants. Both Derek and Nina loved to sit drinking beer before taking the tram back. They had witnessed many amazing performers who ranged from pianists to dancers. That day, their last in Nice, a woman operatic singer appeared, and her strong voice filled the square as she moved from one musical feature to another. Nina went across to place some money in the beautiful, iridescent bowl at her feet. The singer wore a flowing black cape over a full underskirt, held together by a sparkling brooch on one shoulder. The brooch was in the shape of a caduceus. Nina's pulse began to race as she noticed that the tails of the snakes, on the brooch, were intertwined. Just like on her medallion. The woman looked at her as if she knew her and smiled as she held out her hands, her palms facing upwards. Nina backed away, her heart thudding painfully. She sprinted across the square, glancing behind her to see if she was being pursued. The woman stood, still singing the arias into the night air. A sculpture moved towards her, and Nina screamed before realising that it was a performer, one of the many, who regaled the crowd by dressing as marble sculptures. A hand caught her elbow, and she frantically pulled to get away. She whirled around to find Derek looking at her anxiously. People had begun to stare, and Nina shut her eyes as he led her to a chair.

"What's wrong, Nina?"

"Nothing, the man startled me. Let's leave. I have had enough of this place."

She had stubbed her toes against the pavement as she ran, blinded by panic. A nail had cracked halfway down. She examined it briefly before stating, "We forgot to pack band-aids, I need some. This will have to be covered."

Her toe was pulsating with pain but her banal comment was an attempt to regain a sense of normalcy. Her world seemed to have tilted on its axis.

As they walked towards the tramline, Nina examined her response. She was not easily excitable, and yet the thought that she was recognised and had been followed was strangely unsettling. Who were these people claiming her as their kind? Was she the victim of a hoax? Why could she not bring herself to tell Derek what was happening? She told him everything; there were no secrets between them.

The next day they went on a walking tour of the old town, called Vieux Nice and savoured the flavours of Provence. Nina bought some olive oil and perfume from a local perfumery. She was strangely subdued and insisted on returning to their hotel instead of exploring the flower markets as they had planned. Nina was a keen gardener and had wanted to buy bulbs to take back home.

The drugstore in their hotel closed early, so they walked to the big one on the adjoining street. Nina wanted some painkillers. Her toe had begun to throb again. Derek took the alley adjacent to the hotel. It was dark and lonely, except for some young men, who were shouting back and forth to each other. Nina shuddered.

"Are you going down with something? Are you feeling feverish?" Derek wanted to know.

They had emerged into the bright, neon-lit street again. Nina refused to look over her shoulder. She had to get rid of this feeling of being followed. At the drug store, they picked up what they wanted before queuing up. Nina turned her head to see a man, wearing a fitted baseball cap that matched his jacket, looking at her appraisingly. All that week, she had greetings and compliments from men she passed in the street even though Derek was a few paces away. Tall and lissome, with clear, olive skin and dark, liquid eyes, Nina had learned to fend off unwanted attention. She had laughed it off as a part of the local cultural milieu. The man raised his eyebrows and looked at her in a manner that signalled a question. Was she available and willing? Nina looked away; she had avoided making eye contact on the streets of Nice It was read as an invitation to approach. The day's events had erased everything else from her mind. She was bracing herself for the strange encounters which threatened to swamp the even contours of her life. In bracing herself for the unexpected, she had let down her guard. Nina turned away and began to move towards the exit; the unabashed ogling by the French cavaliers which had only amused her earlier, grated on her nerves. To think she had believed she had left behind this show of flagrant, unwanted male attention in India. Turning back to see whether Derek had reached the end of the queue, she collided with someone and would have gone sprawling back had she not been held by a pair of arms. She looked into aquamarine blue eyes, the same that had been watching her a while ago. Pushing back frantically from the grip, she rushed out, and minutes later, Derek joined her. In India, Nina thought she would have known what to do. She felt a rush of panic. The moment they entered the foyer of the hotel, Nina burst into tears. The receptionists looked over at them, glancing sharply at Derek. Once inside their room, Derek pushed Nina into a chair. Plonking himself in front of her, he demanded to know what was the matter. It was unlike Nina to act so skittishly. The story came out between sobs and gasps of breath, slow at first and then in torrents. Derek held her close and then moved back to examine her carefully.

"Where is the chain with the medallion?" he asked tracing her bare neck.

Nina touched her neck. It was not there. A calm had descended on her. It was lost or stolen. The man at the drugstore must have deliberately collided with her. There was no going back, no finding it again.

"Let's search, just once. Retrace our steps. Ask at the drug store."

Nina shuddered. She was exhausted, she just wanted to sleep. Getting into bed, she pulled the covers over her head.

"Exactly like an ostrich," remarked Derek.

"I am going to look for it."

"It's gone," said Nina.

"Never known you to be fatalistic." Derek closed the door behind him.

There was no one in the alley now, it was plunged into darkness. There was no way he could find it there. The people at the drugstore were polite but firm. No lost item had been reported. They obviously did not want to be involved.

Back in their room, he eased himself into bed. Nina was asleep, curled in a foetal position. She turned towards him instinctively, burrowing in as she habitually did. Holding her with both arms, he drew her closer and, it was then that the realisation hit him. The night before, after she had lowered herself onto him and reached down to kiss his mouth, the medallion had jabbed his naked flesh. In a flash, he had pulled it off her. Not wanting to break the rhythm, he reached back to place the medallion on the broad headboard of the bed. The morning had been rushed with them arriving just before the buffet breakfast was cleared. They had hung the 'DO NOT CLEAN' sign on their door handle as Nina had her shopping strewn all over the room. The blue of the day beckoned, and they had walked out into the street without returning to the room. Nina was not particularly observant about things. He wondered whether she had even worn it that day. The next morning would reveal if it had merely fallen into the space under their bed.

Nina woke up with a start. Derek had gone out to the pier. She touched her neck, wishing it had only been a nightmare. She loved that medallion and would pester her mother into letting her wear it even as a child. She was wearing it long before she met Derek. Traditionally, he would have tied a mangal sutra around her neck. That would have replaced the medallion on a chain… or hung along with it thought Nina moodily. Now, it was gone, as if it had never been. She wiped her tears. She did not want to ruin their vacation. It was the first in so many years. She got up to wash away the telltale signs of tears. Derek was turning the key at the door. To her astonishment, he lay on the ground beside the bed and began fishing under it with the hangar he had taken from the wardrobe. Again and again, he pushed his arm as far as it could go. Then he began to move something forward with gentle sweeps of his arm, till finally, it emerged. The caduceus at the end of the chain. Covered with floss and dust, the gems still sparkled. With a whoop of joy, Nina knelt and held it in her palm. Derek knew he would have to confess soon. Right now, he enjoyed her delight.

They would be leaving Nice after lunch. Nina packed hurriedly before sliding beneath the sheets. She would sleep till it was time to go. Derek had offered to do the laundry and avail of the self-laundry option that the accommodation offered. She dreamt of a snake sitting on the window sill of her home; it was shedding its skin.

Chapter III

All Things Bright and Beautiful

Swathed in yellow-gold blossoms that swayed in the caress of the warm breeze and rained down a constant shower of petals, the Cassia Fistula trees seemed constantly in motion. Nina lingered and held out her palm to catch a petal. The ground was carpeted in gold as far as the eye could see. Not long now, thought Nina. Not long before the trees stood denuded of their golden wrapping, having stepped into the fresh, pale green of new growth. This resurrection of the gnarled, old trees of the avenue was a reminder of the ephemeral nature of youth and beauty, in the lesser beings who came to Nina seeking the fountain of youth. Furrowed brows, crowfeet, fine lines and wrinkles were smoothed out, and women gazed at a reflection they never thought would be theirs again. Nina enjoyed watching these women suddenly stand taller and walk out of her clinic, the bounce back in their stride, to take on the world. Her greatest success has been a typist. A brilliant woman, who had chosen to hide her face, pitted and scarred with acne in the dingy confines of a chartered accountant's office. Nina had met her when she had sought help to file her income tax returns and had been impressed by her quiet competence. The girl did not meet her eyes during any of their interactions but just as Nina reached for her bag to leave, she looked up.

Desperately attempting not to flinch when Nina's eyes met hers, she asked, "Can you help me?"

Nina did not pretend that she did not understand her query.

"Yes," she nodded.

"When can we start?"

In her last session with Nina, she spoke about qualifying to become a company secretary. Scars were more than skin deep mused Nina as she took the lift to her clinic, on the topmost floor of one of the city's most prestigious buildings. Scars were corrosive; they burrowed in through the damaged tissues to destroy self-esteem, preventing people from reaching their full potential.

Nina had struggled hard for years to gain acceptance. Living in a country where surgery to correct cleft lips was offered free, but lakhs of children were deprived of corrective surgery because it was ascribed to their karma. Nina had few illusions. She knew that spending money to look good was regarded as an unnecessary indulgence, a prerogative of the rich and the privileged. Though Nina had several celebrity clients, she had made her expertise available to a small percentage of clients for free. There was no system in place to find them. They found her, powered either by a fanatical determination or desperation.

It was three weeks since they had returned to India. Work had claimed them, and after a while, it was like they had never left. Derek was constantly away, supervising environmental projects with impossible deadlines, or fighting the land mafia to stop the silting of lakes. He came home on most days so late that the only meal they shared was breakfast. The trees in the city were festooned with flowers, and Derek was an avid photographer. Ironically, with so much pollen circulation, Derek had a recurrence of a severe respiratory allergy that in no way hampered his sleep. Only the volume of his snores increased by several decibels. Nina escaped into the guest bedroom, stuffing her ears with the earplugs, which she kept handy for just such an occasion. She had taken to watching South Korean serials on Netflix while waiting for Derek to come home. They arrested thoughts, called for a willing suspension of disbelief and sent her to bed dreaming of tall, muscular men who held her in a protective embrace; the kind only the men in Korean dramas seem to have perfected. Derek never hugged unless she initiated it, and then it was a bear hug, so tight, it made her breathless.

October came shrouded in fog. Derek was leaving for Kanha Tiger Reserve. As a chairperson of the advisory committee on Project Tiger in India, it meant a month of touring India's many tiger reserves. Nina was going to her parental home after nearly a year. Almost a decade after leaving home, there were days she so longed to be back that she googled the location of the house, touching it with her fingertips before calling her mother's phone. It felt good to hear her mother's infectious energy come crackling through the uncertain cell phone reception. This time there was an added sense of urgency. She had to learn the story behind the caduceus. She had taken to tucking it out of sight, but the sense of being trailed followed her all the way home to Mysore.

Her parents lived in a farmhouse nestling among an assortment of greenery, hidden by the tall fig trees that spread out their branches as if reaching for the sky. You suddenly happened upon it as you turned the corner. Nina had visualised the last furlong to reach home so many times that it seemed like a refrain. She had refused her mother's offer of their car and had chosen to come home in a taxi. An automatic reflex to her mother's style of hovering motherhood. The entire four hours of the drive had been punctuated by phone calls.

"Yes, momma?"

"Where are you, now? Is there much traffic?"

"Just normal for a Monday."

"Call me when you reach Mandya."

"Okay, amma."

Half an hour later,

"What will you have… rice or chappati? I can make both. Or do you prefer some dosas?"

"Anything will do, ma."

An hour or so later,

"Shall I switch on the geyser? Will you want to bathe?"

"Amma, I am still only halfway. I will call from Mandya. Please don't check on me. The taxi is from a reliable agency, and I am travelling in broad daylight. Please ma, just relax."

The taxi had crossed Mandya, and they were on the road which wound around Kukkarahalli Lake when Nina woke up with a jerk. Her mother would have gone into spasms of panic if she knew Nina had nodded off. At the gate, Nina waited to be greeted by Jiyo, his beautiful muzzle pressed against the bars. She would let him clamber onto her and then reach down to brush her fingers against the white, fork-shaped mark on his forehead. She peered over the gates and saw the porch lights come on. There was a flurry of movements, and her mother arrived breathless and radiant, her silver-white mane like a halo around her head. Just behind her mother came her dad. Quiet to the point of being taciturn, he had been her refuge during her stormy teen years. Cocooned and sheltered, Nina's only grouse had been that her life was too tame. As early as she could, she cut loose and moved away, returning home again and yet again like a migratory bird.

As they walked back together, she gazed at the carefully preserved undergrowth among which a variety of fruit trees grew. Their bounty filled her mother's kitchen shelf with an assortment of jams, preserves and pickles.

Later that night, after her mother had finally gone to bed, Nina found herself lying wide-eyed and awake. Her muscles ached, and it was with a whoosh of pleasure that she had sunk into the mattress. "Too soft", she could hear Derek say. "Bad for your spine." But it felt so peaceful to be enfolded and held snugly under the patchwork comforter made from bits and pieces of her infant clothes. Outside the window, the butter fruit tree traced a delicate tapestry of shapes against the sheer curtains. Something flitted past. A nightjar, perhaps?

A short, harsh screech from the tree announced a spotted owlet. The butter fruit tree had harboured many an avian life. Her mother, a closet poet, had written a poem that Nina remembered with ease. Titled 'conception', it always made Nina happy as she visualized the tree in her mind's eye. She whispered the lines softly.

I saw the butter fruit tree

Spring into comely shape

rain snuffed out the light

the tree moved in rhythm

embraced by pounding gust

it swayed back and forth,

knew a strange, wild rapture

the sap oozed, then erupted

in a swift orgasmic surge

then grew still, quiescent.

In the half-light, glistened

its pale limbs, lay abandoned

toes splayed, the ripples fading.

Warmed by the sun, burgeoned.

The rounded trunk displayed

a glowing cluster, amid leaves,

starry shapes that slowly grew

bulbous and fleshy; the fruit

of a frenzied, fleeting moment

the memory of inescapable joy,

a storm, fierce and turbulent

now, nascent, tremulous life.

Chapter IV

An Encounter in the Hometown and a Journey

Sitting on stone steps leading down to the Kukkarahalli Lake, Nina felt her mind enter that restful state where all that pervaded her consciousness was the rippling, silver sheet of water. There was a plonk close by as a darter raised its snake-like neck before diving in. It came up again, a few yards away with something in its beak, before vanishing into the lake's mysterious depths. Nina trained her binoculars at the bird island. Her trained eyes had caught a glimpse of the painted stork among the pelicans and the spot-billed ducks. All through school and even while pursuing a course in liberal arts at a local college, Nina had been a member of the amateur bird watcher's group. They had compiled a list of migratory birds which visited the lake, and more than a few on the list were spotted by Nina. She had that quick vision and the ability, referred to as 'jizz' among bird watchers, to know the identity of a bird from obscure characteristics. Jizz probably would have started as, "it just is". You knew from years of observation that a shape vaguely outlined, moving like an arrow, was a horn-bill. Nina knew even when being awoken from a slumber that a curlew was flying past. Their high-pitched calls sounded forlorn. As a child, Nina had imagined them flying to strange, magical lands, far away from human habitation. For her, bird watching was no mere pursuit, it was a lifelong habit; something she unconsciously did.

Her stomach gave a rumble, a reminder that her mother would be peering out of the window with breakfast in mind. Scurrying out at dawn, to get ahead of the regular walkers around the lake, she had forgotten to carry her phone. But she had carried her camera and captured plenty of beautiful, grey and white images of the lake on a cloudy morning. Dusting the back of her trousers and stretching luxuriously, she began jogging slowly back to the promenade. It was crowded. The stretch ahead to the promenade had fewer walkers. A man ran past wearing bermudas, a cap shading his eyes from the sun. Another firangi in Mysore to learn yoga, she thought. He would learn to cover up soon. Kukkarahalli mosquitoes loved white skin as did most of India. Nina stopped to see a pond heron duck quickly into the vegetation before her camera got it in focus.

A pond heron was not a shy creature. Something must have frightened it. Was that moving log a crocodile? The purple swamp hens were retreating in panic. She raised her binoculars, but not before she had caught sight of the same man, the foreigner, running past again. He was not looking her way. How did he reappear so fast? The embankment around the lake was circular, and it took thirty minutes to complete a run around the lake. He must have run through the small patch of wilderness on the left of the embankment. She hastened her steps unconsciously, walking towards the promenade. Someone else was approaching from the opposite direction; a man running swiftly towards her. She shifted away from his path and slowed her pace. The bund, which went all around the lake, was narrow at that point., She would have to pass close to him. He was looking at her directly. Jizz. Her heart froze as she met eyes of aquamarine blue, and then he ran past colliding into someone just behind her. She turned around to see the man in the bermudas hit the ground with a thud before she began to race, up the slope, towards where she could see a crowd gathering. People ran past her towards where the two men, in what seemed like an embrace, had gone toppling down the steep wall of the embankment, into the water below. Nina thought of that log in the water, which had lurched forward. A crocodile? Would the men escape those gaping jaws? She shuddered her imagination on an overdrive. What was happening? Why had the man in the bermudas returned once again? He seemed to have been running in circles around her. The other man was not a stranger. She had seen him in Nice. He must have followed her to Mysore... right into her sanctuary. She knew intuitively that the collision she had witnessed had to do with the caduceus; with her possession of it. She felt excited and frightened at the same time. There was no easy way out. She would have to tread a path, shrouded in the fog of time.

Nina knew she would have to tease information out of her mother without arousing her suspicion. Her mother was an overly protective parent. Nina had tried everything, from subterfuge to confrontation, to escape her near-constant vigil as a teenager. There were days when she would ride her bike to the top of the Chamundi Hills with her group of friends. The steep road and the sheer precipice on either side had added a sense of adventure to what she regarded as a tame existence.

Now adventure had found her. Ironically, handed over by her mother, tissue-wrapped, in a jewel box.

The next day, her mother was assisting a stray bitch in labour. A vet by profession, Shanti had adopted all stray creatures in her neighbourhood. Or rather they had found their way to her. Abandoned kittens were left on her window sill, and they became so numerous that the farm had begun to represent a mini jungle, with feline creatures curled up at various vantage points. Sturdy pillars dotted the farm, with pedestals to place the birdbaths; their lower end wrapped in sharply -spiked wire to prevent predation. The farm had known only one dog, Jiyo. He had come into their home and hearts wrapped in blue. Jiyo was a mutt, born to a beautiful Maltese mother, who had sneaked off for a romantic rendezvous with an Indian pariah dog. Just like in Nina's favourite animation, The Lady and the Tramp. Nina believed that her love for the story had conjured it to life. The result of the unconventional affair was two pups, one which favoured the mother with an all-white coat and the other was a black, male pup. It had stray bits of a warm brown and a long, extended streak of white running down its forehead. When he looked at Nina with his toffee-brown eyes, she lost her heart to him, and he came home bundled in the baby blanket her mother had preserved for posterity. Nina named him 'Jiyo', which in Hindi meant live long. And that he did, guarding them zealously against snakes and all human marauders. To her chagrin, he hated her friends and would act in the most offish manner, baring his teeth, the ruff standing up behind his neck. She would lock him up in their car shed where he would run back and forth, literally gnashing his teeth. When he finally had to be put to rest after a period of prolonged illness, Nina's mother took her for a drive. In later years Nina could never recall the events of that day… only the sense of a sunless day and pain like a tight knot in her throat which she could not cough up. Her mother watched with dismay as her child grieved. She encouraged her to take up Salsa dancing, for the first time putting aside her fear of Nina entering a world she was unacquainted with. Youth is resilient, and Nina seemed to recover though she never again agreed to keep a pet. Years later, Nina's mother discovered a diary, where Nina had recorded her heartbreak, and realised that it was journalling that had kept her child sane.

Coming up behind her mother, who was turning the late gooseberries into an instant pickle, Nina reached across and plucked a piece. She sucked on it with intense pleasure; it was tart and fiery. She was about to reach for another, but her mother swatted her hand away. Nina remembered. Pickles, according to her mother, turned bad if you touched them with your hand. Turning away to fetch a spoon, Nina asked,

"Amma, do you have a saree to go with this?"

She pulled out the caduceus.

"What is the occasion?"

"When is Onam? I thought I would just fly out to Kodungallur for Onam?"

"Alone?"

"What do you mean? Didn't I come here, ALONE?"

"I meant, is Derek coming?"

"No, he isn't. Perhaps later, I haven't checked. I just feel like it. And we have never been there for the festival."

"Okay, I will come."

"No, you won't. Perhaps, we can go together another time. How will appa manage without you, even for a few days? He cannot take care of your menagerie."

It annoyed Nina that her mother felt that she still needed an escort.

Her normally ebullient mother was quiet. Nina knew, without being told, that her mother was thinking of the days it would detract from her stay with them.

"You had better check, Nina. The old tharavadu is in shambles and a new house is just being built."

Her mother turned away with a sigh and began wiping the pickle jars with care.

"I will need a saree. Which one will go with this?"

Her mother didn't spare a second glance…"You will need a few for the temples."

The temples in Kerala did not allow women wearing pants or churidars to enter. As a child, Nina had been aghast when her mother whisked off her churidar and stuffed it into her bag as they waited, in a queue, to enter the sanctum sanctorum of the Guruvayur temple. She would probably have thrown a tantrum but for the curious onlookers.

Nina watched as her mother began spooning the pickle into sparkling, crystal jars.

"Ma does this piece of jewellery have any special significance?"

"It's an amulet, given to the eldest, girl child in the family."

"Why that?"

"For the continuation of the family name."

"Suppose there are no children?"

"Why would I suppose that?"

Before the conversation turned to her mother's constant refrain about it being time Derek and Nina started a family, Nina asked,

"Who did this belong to originally?"

"You are going there. Find out. But, why the sudden interest?"

Her mother paused in the task of bottling the pickles and looked at her, scrutinising her face carefully. That was a look Nina dreaded. Her mother's antenna to sniff out the truth was out and waving.

"Arre, I wear it, all the time. People ask you know. Do you even know what this symbol is?" Nina asked, brandishing the pendant under her mother's nose.

"It is a caduceus."

"What?". The question came out like a shot.

Startled, her mother, Shanti turned around and looked at her strangely.

"A caduceus."

"Tell me more."

Shanti sighed. She could never understand this child of hers. She had better tell her all she knew. There was something Nina was hiding, but she would tell her, only when she would tell her. Meanwhile, Shanti had no defences against her pester power.

"The caduceus is an ancient Greek symbol. In America, they use it as a symbol of the healing power of medicine. That actually began with an error."

"I didn't know that… well?"

Her mother grinned

"They confused the caduceus with the staff of Aesculapius… trust them to get it wrong."

"How?"

"They mistook the caduceus for the serpent-entwined rod of the Greek god of healing, Aesculapius. They used two intertwined serpents on the symbol instead of one. The caduceus instead of the rod of Aesculapius, the god of healing and medicine."

"Ma, what is on this?"

"It is the caduceus."

"Haven't you noticed a difference?"

Her mother placed the lid back on the last pickle jar and carefully wiped the oil streaks along the rim. Then she peered at the jewellery.

"The tails are tied in a knot. An adaptation designed by the jeweller. I hardly ever wore it, Nina. It's a pretty piece though, and you always fancied it… with so many colours of gems, you can wear it with almost everything."

Nina called Derek that night to tell him about the change in her plans. He wanted her to come back. They could resolve the mystery later. She had to exercise caution. He would have come. Impossible now. The tiger population in Kanha Tiger Reserve had taken a hit when two males in their prime died of unknown causes. The Chief Minister's office had spoken directly to him.

"The old house is going to be pulled down, Derek. It is now or never. I feel I must know. I will never feel really safe again, even if we keep the pendant in a locker."

On her last day, Nina took her parents to one of Mysore's most iconic hotels, The Green Hotel. It was mentioned in 'The Lonely Planet' and got throngs of visitors, from all over the world, every year. The former residence of a princess of the royal family of Wodeyars, the hotel was a lovely white building with a lush, flower-bordered garden. There were white, wicker chairs in the open area and rather shabby but genteel antique furnishing in the enclosed dining spaces. The menu was unchanging, but a very genial manager went around enquiring about the gustatory needs of the guests. Food was tweaked to the preference of the guests. This rare, personal touch and an excellent bakery were among the many features which made the hotel so popular with both the local residents and the tourists.

It was cool under the shade of the trees as they walked to the enclosed, outer dining space of the hotel. Though the place was already crowded, the head waiter led them to an arrangement of seats in the corner. Their family were among the regular patrons, and Nina felt welcomed by the smiles of recognition she received from the waiters scurrying past, all dressed in green. The Green Hotel took pride in living up to its name by using solar energy, and they used recycled water for the garden. The interiors were designed using Indian crafts and employing traditional craftsmen, many of whom were National Award winners.

Without glancing at the menu, they ordered plates of gobi-manchurian and a pitcher of beer. Shifting slightly so that she could see the others in the room, Nina locked eyes with a man staring at her from the next table. She had never seen him before, but the expression in his eyes was unmistakable. He held her eyes, and for a moment the rest of the room faded as he looked, his admiration like a warm current that connected them. Then someone spoke, her mother perhaps, and Nina sank back into her chair, shutting out the room. Her heart was thudding in her ears, and she flushed with embarrassment.

Nina did not want dessert, but her parents ate with obvious relish from the platter of pastries. As they walked towards their sedan, parked under a clump of trees, Nina thought she saw a glint of glass from the upper windows of the hotel. Someone was looking out of the window with a pair of binoculars. She felt oddly vulnerable as they drove away. The peaceful, little city, a euphemism for an overgrown village, had suddenly turned hostile.

She took the Monday morning Indigo flight from Mysore to Cochin. She wore the pendant, shortening the adjustable chain till it hung just below the hollow of her neck. She was certain that she was being watched and wanted to fend off attacks on the farmhouse. Would they go so far? Who were they? Keeping the chain short gave less room for a chain snatcher to grab it, in the passing. There were not many people in the small airport, but there was a girl she recognised, in a young, boisterous group. Unhurriedly, she made her way to them. They were students, of the All India Institute of Speech and Hearing, on their way to attend a conference. She sat with them till the flight was announced. Since the airport was a small one, the aircraft landed nearby, and the passengers walked a short distance to board their flights. As soon as boarding was announced, Nina wound a scarf around her neck and stepped out just ahead of the students. She was certain of nothing now; staying alert was her best defence till she had unravelled it all.

The takeoff was delayed by fifteen minutes after all the passengers were seated. Then, some people entered speaking French. Nina, who had taken the advanced level course of French at the Alliance Francaise, could understand that the group was heading for the Jewish settlement in Kochi. Something stirred, it was like a prompt she did not want to register. Takeoffs always made her queasy, and so she had laid her head against the back of the seat and put a mask over her eyes. Suddenly restless, she slipped the mask and opened her eyes. He was looking at her, frozen in the act of putting his baggage in the overhead compartment. The man whose naked admiration had left her aroused and flustered. This time, his features were composed, but his eyes lit up in recognition. Nina looked away and quickly put the mask back before averting her face. She must have nodded off. The next thing she knew was the air hostess requesting her to pull up the window shutter since landing was in progress. Of her admirer, there was no sign and her favourite cousin, Roy, stepped out of the crowd to hug her and trundle her suitcase along. Roy was short for Rohan, his mother preferring an anglicized version. He looked a lot older since she had last seen him. Roy now sported a full beard and had wound his hair into a man bun.

As they raced along the highway, Nina let out a few gasps of sheer panic. There were private buses and lorries, competing with the usual motley stream of traffic. They all seemed collision-bound, and Nina felt her stomach heave, just the way it did when she had gone on a roller-coaster ride. That never-to-be-repeated ride. So severe had Nina's reaction been that for a few months, she could not ride on an elevator without feeling her insides plummeting. Sensing her discomfort, Roy slowed down. He was soon distracting her with good-humoured gossip about the family, and some rather outrageous tales about his own amorous adventures. The landscape was changing, the earth a deep, red colour in sharp contrast to the fecund green which grew luxuriantly to the very edge of the asphalted roads. It had been years since her last visit, but the very smell of the place, a woody smell redolent of the sap coursing through the massive trees and the green fields of rice, saturated the air. Soon, they were turning into the lane leading to her mother's ancestral home. The lane was narrow, and Roy slowed down to allow a cyclist to scrape past their car. The woven fences of coconut leaves, on either side of the road, had been replaced by walls. Roy had to reverse before they swept along a long, narrow stretch with the old home standing in magnificent splendour, facing the drive. Her mother's cousin, Maya, stood waiting for her at the door. Her face beamed with delight as she ran down the steps to embrace Nina. Her eyes were filled with moisture which she did not attempt to wipe as she held Nina away and exclaimed, "How beautiful you have grown. You look like Shanti of course, but really, you are the spitting image of Nani Kutty."

Nani Kutty was a celebrated beauty of her times. Her painting hung in the gallery of photographs, of both the dead and the living, in the central hall of the house. Nina paused to gaze at her. She had been painted in the glory of her motherhood with her numerous progenies, gathered in a circle, around her feet. Her face was arresting, and the onlooker was compelled to gloss over the details, to gaze in fascination at eyes which blazed out, as if she was about to vent some deeply buried emotion. Nina shook her head and followed Maya, whom she addressed as chechi, into the bedroom which was always allotted to a member of the family returning to their tharavadu home.

Nani Kutty had lived a sedate life. Living in times where it was nothing out of the ordinary for a Nair woman to live with more than one partner in a lifetime, Nani Kutty had married early, known only one spouse and raised eight children. That, Nina thought must have won her much accolade. Nani Kutty had no siblings but she had ensured that the seeds of the family tree were dispersed multiple times. Nina's grandmother had been her last child and had come two years after Nani Kutty had ceased menstruating. She had been regarded as a miracle baby, all the more for being unexpected. Maya chechi was a natural chronicler of events. Nina hoped she could get some insight into the origin of the medallion. She would have to delve deep into events of the past before their long shadows cast a shade on her life.

The house was large and sprawling with a wooden ceiling and shining, black stone floors. A long shrub-lined driveway led to the rather imposing front door. On the southern side of the house was a veranda with a low wall flanked and supported by columns. You could sit on it for an intimate moment with a favoured cousin or lie back staring up at the deep blue of the sky. As a child, Nina had spent hours staring at the floating clouds passing like a pageant. Gazing had a soporific effect and she dozed till she was startled awake by a concerned relative, scolding her for sleeping on the narrow ledge of the wall.

Nina was given a room, the windows of which faced the veranda beyond which she could see the pond which she had loved to wade in, as a child. There were tiny silverfish in the pond, which nibbled at the toes and tickled them when you stood still. Now, the pond was flanked by vegetation so thick that it was hardly visible except in breaks between the foliage, where it shimmered green. With dusk, the palms in the coconut grove cast menacing shadows which seem to draw closer. Nina shut the window. The room smelt fetid. The old tharavadu was dying. She would have to hurry to listen to its last, whispered confessions.

Chapter V

There is Something in the Attic

Nina tossed for a long time listening to the grandfather clock, in the hallway, striking the hours. The pedestal fan in the room barely stirred the sultry, warm air. There was a short, sharp shower which finally brought some respite, and Nina fell into a deep sleep until woken by the clamour, just outside her bedroom window. For a panic-stricken moment, she could not recall where she was, and then she recognised Maya chechi's voice raised several octaves above normal. She threw open her windows to see Maya chechi gesticulating wildly. Nina ran out to the small group of people, who had gathered, skidding on something wet and slippery. It was a small, grey fish. Roy was leading Maya back towards their home, holding her firmly by the arm. Seeing Nina, Maya burst into angry, incoherent speech.

Nina caught the tail end, "rascals, may they rot like fish."

"The lucky bastards are probably enjoying a redolent breakfast of yam and fish," laughed Roy.

"Why is fish strewn everywhere?" asked Nina in bewilderment.

She could see the onlookers, probably neighbours, picking fish and stuffing it into the folds of the waist cloth, the mundu, which was tied halfway up to form a bag.

"Rascals," said the usually serene Maya, frothing at the mouth.

It was Roy who explained to Nina, between guffaws, that they had been robbed. The pond was being used for fish farming in recent years. Under the cover of darkness, the fish had been hauled out of the water in cast nets. In making their escape, the thieves must have slipped, strewing a bit of the catch around. While Maya bridled at the impertinence of the thieves, Roy was hugely amused. Not the best of times to seek answers to mysteries thought Nina.

After breakfast, Nina called Derek. His phone was out of range, which was not unusual when he was in the forest reserves. Nina felt a familiar sense of annoyance well up within her. He had not called even to find out whether she had landed safely. She chucked the phone into her bag and went in search of Maya chechi. Nina discovered her sitting, legs outstretched, stringing flowers. She smiled warmly at Nina.

"Do you want some tender coconut water? It's so sultry! Monsoon is poor this year."

Maya wiped the perspiration beading her forehead.

"No chechi. Puttu-kadala and pappadam are very filling. I feel like a python which has swallowed its prey".

"You are too thin… and you look tired."

"Chechi, I will never be a plump, buxom Kerala beauty."

"Haven't you seen the new breed of Malayali beauties on the screen? They look like waifs… all with bobbed hair. None of them has your long, thick mane. You are the true Kerala beauty. The spitting image of Nani Kutty."

The conversation had veered back to Nani Kutty. Seeing an opening, Nina asked,

"I have never heard about Nani Kutty's siblings?"

"Nani Kutty's mother was married twice, the second time to a paralysed man."

"And the first? What happened to him."

"He went back to Greece."

"You mean, Nani Kutty's father was Greek?"

"Who knows for sure? Her mother married her cousin, even before a month was over. He became paralysed, soon afterwards, in an accident. As a paraplegic, could he have fathered a child?"

"Yes. Even quadriplegics can have sex. So, we really don't know, do we?"

There was silence as they brooded about the question.

"What about children from her first marriage? Were there none? Maya chechi, help me know?"

"Why Nina? Why now? Haven't you heard? Let the dead past bury its dead," said Maya who had taught English literature before she retired from the University.

"Because of this," said Nina pulling out the medallion.

Maya listened, at first with fascination and later with a growing look of anxiety. Nina related the strange encounters and her suspicion that they all led back to the caduceus.

"Let's start with the boxes in the attic. There are writings on palm leaves which no one has bothered to study. I wanted to after I retired. That never happened. They must be moth-eaten by now."

Nina had never dared venture into the attic as a child. She had been warned of civet cats that lived in the attic and took pleasure in devouring little girls. In lambing season, the lambs used to be brought into the house at night and tied at the bottom of the stairs leading to the attic. This was to ward off attacks from jackals and other predators. Nina would refuse to sleep till the attic door was firmly shut and latched. She had visions of the civet cats making a meal of the lambs. She had explored it as a teenager but found that the low roof and the heat it trapped made it too uncomfortable to linger long.

Maya had the huge, iron trunks brought down from the attic. There were some old novels, mostly tales of the Wild West and detective novels featuring Perry Mason. Nina had always been a compulsive reader. She picked up a Zane Grey novel and began to flip through the yellowing pages. It was one of her favourites. She had devoured them as an adventure-hungry youngster. Now, reading 'To the Last Man', she grew absorbed and Maya found her, leaning against the wall, completely lost to her surroundings. With a sigh, Maya dragged a stool and began rummaging through the contents, throwing them into a heap. Right at the very bottom was a bundle, wrapped in yellow cloth bearing the symbol of the caduceus. She heard Nina take a sharp intake of breath.

"That's the insignia…"

Nina swooped it up opening it like a gift.

She unravelled a long piece of cloth.

"That looks like the bit of a sail."

Inside was something, wrapped in oilcloth. Very gently, Nina opened and squatting down, spread out two bundles of palm-leafed documents.

She looked at Maya chechi, her eyes wide with anticipation. Maya chechi examined the bundles.

"They are well preserved. Let's not open them yet. I know Prof. Shankar Menon. He is the Director of the International Centre for Culture and Heritage. He will help us."

The Centre was closed for Onam vacation, so they would have to wait.

Nina had no time to chafe; the preparations for Onam were in full swing. Maya had called several of her neighbours, almost all of whom were related to them. They were a vast clan and Nina had never really got to meet them all, on their brief trips to Kerala, when her grandmother was alive. These trips had stopped altogether when her parents' professional commitments grew, and Nina left for the University. Nina had never felt she had missed out on siblings; she had enjoyed being an only child till her teen years. Then, she suddenly turned claustrophobic and felt smothered. Her parents had let her go knowing that like migratory birds, children return. The direction back, they knew, was chartered by love and not possessive restraint.

After helping Maya draw a large pookolam, an intricate design of multi-hued flower petals, Nina went to check on the enticing aromas wafting from the kitchen. While the house had a kitchen with a hob and gas connection, there was a separate building at the back for cooking food over wood fires. Traditionally, the cooks employed to prepare a feast were male. Men, stripped to their waist, were scraping coconuts into snowy heaps, while still others were cutting up vegetables at a speed which signalled no interruption. As a child, Nina was allowed to wander around and often got treated to the rich payasam. But, a woman amidst their solemn endeavour was not welcome. The chef looked up from his boiling cauldron and waved her away. Feeling awkward, Nina moved away. She knew it was nothing personal. It had to do with the belief that a woman was impure if she was of the age to be menstruating. That was something so deeply entrenched in the socio-religious fabric of the place that no amount of modernity could erase it.

The guests had begun to arrive. Nina could hear Maya chechi's voice ringing as she called out greetings. There was a rumble of voices from the rooms in front as guests continued to arrive. Tucking a string of jasmine into her long braid, Nina checked herself in the full-length mirror. Her settu mundu was pinned securely, and there would be no wardrobe malfunction when she squatted for a meal. Her appearance was greeted with silence and then everyone began to speak at once. She responded to the babble of questions in Malayalam that sounded strange even to her ears. Yes, her mother was well. No, she had not accompanied her. Her husband would not be coming either, this time. To her relief, Maya chechi came and called them into the long hall where plantain leaves were placed, on the gleaming, black floor, for the feast. Nina found herself seated next to a woman, who looked like an octogenarian. She had watched as Maya chechi had offered the woman a seat, at the dining table where some of the older guests were seated.

The old woman had turned and pointed towards where Nina was seated. Before Maya chechi could respond, she walked across the room with an agility that belied her age and sat next to Nina. Turning to her she said, "You are said to be the replica of Nani Kutty. Nani Kutty was more beautiful."

"How so?" asked Nina, amused by her companion's forthrightness.

"Fairer with poocha kannu."

Cat's eyes meant green eyes, of course. Nina turned in surprise. "They look black in the picture… and how do you know?"

"The artist painted them black. Poocha kannu was not admired in those days."

Turning to Nina she added, "I played with your grandmother, you know."

"So, you actually saw Nani Kutty?"

Her elderly companion ignored the question and added, "Your hair is like that of your tharavadu women. Long, black and lustrous. Nani Kutty had hair as brown as the coconut husk."

"So, I am more beautiful," asserted Nina triumphantly. The next moment she was groaning at the sight of the second serving of the gooey, utterly delicious, jackfruit payasam that had been ladled onto her leaf while she was distracted. There was no way she could eat anymore.

Noticing her expression, the woman added,

"Eat it with a pappadam. A little more flesh will make your husband happy."

The woman was smiling now, her teeth edged with the stain of betel leaf.

He probably will not notice thought Nina. Unless I am a tigress in Sariska.

Taking a stab in the dark, she added

"Wasn't her father a Greek mariner?"

"I heard that he was a videshi. Nani Kutty's mother married twice. The second time to a karnavar of your family. Nani Kutty was born eight months later. Nobody believed she was his child."

"How do you know that?"

The woman said, "I am Kartyayani, the daughter of Kalyani Amma. My grandmother was the midwife who was summoned when Ammini Amma went into labour. My mother was a little girl at that time. She had tagged along and was present at Nani Kutty's birth. The child was born full-term. The labour was short. Ammini Amma, Nani Kutty's mother, must have had children before. We are a family of midwives… we are trained when young and know many secrets…" Her voice trailed off. She pinched her lips and looked away.

Nina was too startled to say anything further. Kartyayani was lying on her side on the floor. Nina knew this was to continue with the repast after she had recovered. There were many such prone figures in the room. Social etiquette did not permit a guest to resume eating if they left to wash. So, it was customary for people to rest alongside their leaves, for a while, before having a few more helpings of dessert.

Seeing that people had begun to rise, Nina got up and went to wash her hands. She would talk to Kartyayani Amma later. She hovered around the room waiting, but Kartyayani Amma seemed to have fallen asleep. Her phone rang. Derek, at last. The reception on the phone was poor. She could hardly hear him. He would be back home in a week. When did she plan on coming home? She did not know. Before she could speak further, the call got disconnected. She tried to call back a couple of times, but clearly, he was out of range, once again.

Nina hunted frantically, but Kartyayani Amma had disappeared. Most of the guests had left. Maya chechi, Roy told her, was in the kitchen distributing the leftovers. It was there that Nina saw Kartyayani Amma in the company of a buxom, young woman who was leading her out. Nina stopped to talk to her, but Kartyayani Amma merely stared back at her with vacant eyes. Her companion smiled pleasantly and said,

"Ammuma has dementia. I saw her next to you at the feast. But now she is tired. What did you want to ask her?"

"Nothing much. She did say she was my grandmother's friend and even remembers my great-grandmother."

"She has sudden flashes of memory. Mostly, about the times she was a child. But she cannot remember even whether she has eaten. I have to hasten before she begins to ask for food again. She can be quite violent if we don't comply with her demands."

Nina was in a quandary. The woman had dementia. Could she believe her? She would wait for any evidence the palm leaf manuscripts provided before confiding in Maya chechi. No children were considered illegitimate in the Nair book of ethics. Since they traced the family lineage from the women in the family, there were no bastard children. However, promiscuity was frowned upon here as elsewhere. Relationships were monogamous. But a widow or a woman who had been abandoned could marry again. While Ammini Amma's act of seeking a guardian for her child was unquestionable, there were too many blanks in the story. Nina wanted to find the answers before confiding in anyone.

Prof. Shankar Menon responded promptly. The manuscripts were in two languages, Greek and Malayalam. Since they were well preserved and not very long, there was no difficulty digitising them. He would send the digitised versions within a week.

Chapter VI

Maya

The insignificant envelope addressed to Mrs. Maya Menon lay in the post box along with the water bill, a pamphlet from the Nair association and a small, dark gecko which Nina mistook for a twig. Reaching in gingerly, Nina drew the envelope out and hastened into the house, her heart racing. The sender was Prof. Shankara Menon. She ran into the room where Maya chechi was seated, at the dining table, slicing through a mound of mangoes with finesse a cordon bleu would envy. Startled by Nina's approach, she turned, her knife slashing through the air. Nina stepped back. Maya chechi's eyes looked menacing behind the glasses, her stance that of a fighter. Seeing Nina cringe with fear, Maya chechi lowered her arm with a half-laugh.

"Where did you learn that?" asked Nina.

"It's a stance used in Kalari fight."

"You learnt Kalari?"

"For eight years."

"You were scary. I thought for a moment..."

"That I was going to attack?" Living in this mouldering, old home alone, anything unfamiliar brings out instincts which I thought were lost."

Maya had lost her husband to non-alcoholic liver cirrhosis barely a year ago.

Nina held out the envelope and watched as Maya chechi slit it open.

"Is it from who I think it is?" asked Nina, her voice quivering with excitement.

Maya chechi passed the single, white sheet she had drawn out to Nina, who ran her eyes down it. Then, both women rose in unison and began to run towards Roy's room. The note was brief to the point of being terse.

Dear Maya,

The contents of both palm-leaf manuscripts are interesting, though rather personal. My computer was hacked. I suppose, there is no connection to this task that you entrusted me. I am not taking any chances. So, instead of mailing the digitised version to your niece, I have sent it in a pen drive with Roy. I met him at one of his favourite haunts. Roy knows nothing. He merely thinks these are some files of the conference we chaired a few months ago.

Regards,

Shankar.

Roy inhabited the two-roomed, semi-detached apartment opening onto the terrace, during the day. It was his lair. His friends came and left without accessing the main house. Since Maya was alone, he chose to sleep in the main house at night. Today, he was nowhere to be found. Tearing up the stairs, ahead of Maya chechi, Nina nearly tripped over his helmet. Both women were brought up short by the sight of the terrace door left wide open. The door of Roy's room was ajar, and Roy lay sprawled over the bed, one foot resting on the floor. Had he been struck with a weapon, wondered Nina. The room looked ransacked with contents spilling out of drawers. Maya chechi peered at Roy and drew back hastily, covering her nose with the end of her saree. Fearing the worst, Nina asked,

"What's it, chechi? Is Roy hurt?"

"Drunk senseless. Not hurt. He will get hurt plenty when he wakes up."

Maya chechi grabbed the clothes strewn on the floor. She began to go through the pockets of the pants he had worn, which lay in the heap at the foot of the bed, before throwing it away. It fell at Nina's feet with a clunk. Nina lifted it gingerly; it had a distinctly male odour and looked unwashed. Feeling along the sides, she traced the outlines of some object lying just in the pockets. When she slid her hand in, there was nothing. Just something that looked like a decorative braid. It had a tiny head. A zip? Nina pulled it delicately down. With one finger, she gently eased out two pen drives, hardly bigger than her thumb.

"Maya chechi, look."

Maya chechi got off the floor with a sigh.

"At least, he had the sense to stow them away secretly."

"But", interrupted Nina, "someone just broke in. Shouldn't we call the police? Or alert neighbours?"

Maya chechi laughed, "Roy's room always looks as if it has been burgled. He thrives on chaos. There must be a method in his madness. But, unlike Hamlet, there is no Ophelia on the scene. Maybe, a shrew will tame him."

"Quoting Shakespeare or rather misquoting him, makes for weird conversation," continued Maya chechi. "A carry-over from my university days."

"Let's view it together. Shall we?" asked Nina. She had not heard a word. Her senses heightened with excitement as she felt the minuscule pen drives, she held, burn her palm.

"You go ahead. Tell me what you learn. Today I have to offer prayers at the sarpakava."

The sarpakava was a sacred grove, allowed to run wild. A space dedicated as the abode of the snake, it was enclosed by huge trees over which grew interwoven, giant creepers. Their foliage created a bower through which the sun's rays could not quite penetrate. The resultant light was green with impenetrable shadows. Maya rarely went there except to light a lamp on special days and place milk in front of the idol of Nagaraja. Her husband had been a rationalist, who had refused to pay obeisance to any god. Maya was not pious, but she liked to adhere to certain practices. As a naturalist, she knew the importance of preserving an ecosystem that sustained myriad forms of life. Maya's eyes never left the ground as she walked slowly, banging the floor of the forest with a stick. Snakes sensed the vibrations and moved away. The grove was swarming with snakes, and occasionally, Maya had to dodge a branch on which a splendid specimen lay sunning. She had reached the heart of the grove. Here the light filtering through the branches was a translucent green, giving the scene a surrealistic feel. Maya bent her head before the stone representations of Nagaraja surrounded by other Naga devatas and placed the lamp, along with a bowl of water. It was customary to offer milk, but Maya had read that snakes do not drink milk. She knew they drank water. She had watched a snake from her kitchen window drink from the birdbath. It took swallows of water like a thirsty human would. She caught a flicker of movement, behind a fallen log, from the corner of her eyes. All her senses on alert, she swung around. There was someone else in the grove besides her. The muscles at the back of her neck bunched up, and there was a tingling along her spine. Slowly, scythe in hand, she drew near the log. The scythe, she used for splitting ripe jackfruit open, was held aloft, ready to cleave through yielding flesh. In the gathering gloom, she was a sight to strike fear; an avenging goddess. A log came hurtling towards her as a man sprang backwards. Maya threw the scythe at him, deeply-honed instincts taking over. The projectile hit the fleeing figure between the shoulder blades. The man stumbled, and then with a bound, he jumped over the fence beyond which lay a rainwater canal. Maya paused. Swinging around on her heels, she surveyed the grove for other presences, and then with rapid strides which belied her age walked out into the clearing beyond the grove.

"Help, thief," she shouted again and again in a voice that rang through the neighbourhood.

The response to her summons was instantaneous. Within minutes men and women came, and search parties swept through the adjoining thickets in the direction she had pointed. There had been paltry thefts in the neighbourhood. Clothes hung out to dry or some ripening fruit, but the big one had been the theft of fish from Maya thampuratti's pond.

Nina was running a scan on the pen drives when she heard Maya chechi call out. Her heart froze. Had trouble followed in her wake? Pushing the pen drives into the cleft between her breasts, she rose. The act was primordial and instinctive... many generations of women had hidden secrets there to escape detection.

Maya was emphatic. She had prevented another plunder of fish from the other pond. The one which lay at the extreme end of their house was teeming with carefully cultured marine life. The man she had wounded must have come for it. Nina did not dare confide her fear that the appearance of an intruder in the sarpakava was linked to her possession of the caduceus. The caduceus was like a magnet attracting encounters with strange people. Maya chechi would mount a guard on her with Roy in attendance. Where was Roy anyway? He had not made his appearance amid all the noise and frantic activity.

"Roy," called Maya chechi not bothering to mount the stairs again.

Nina volunteered to go and fetch Roy. The room looked just the same, and Roy lay unmoving, spread-eagled over the bed. He had shifted his position, which was reassuring. Nina shook him in vain. Finally, she splashed water, and it was then that he heaved into life. Pushing Nina, in his hasty scramble to the toilet, he began to throw up. As spasms shook his body, Nina rubbed his back. She gagged, reeling back from the reek of alcohol and stale, undigested food. Roy pushed her out and turned on the cold shower. It was a while before he emerged, shaking droplets of water like a mastiff, a half-grin pasted on his face. Responding to Nina's look of enquiry, Roy brought his hands together in a namaste and said,

"Don't tell amma."

"Roy?"

"This has never happened before. I swear someone must have mixed the drinks."

"Your friends?"

"Nope, not likely. It must be that waiter at the bar I argued with."

"Why Roy? Not like you at all."

Even as she said that Nina realised that she knew nothing about Roy. It was just polite talk on her part.

"I swear he was waiting to pick my pocket. He bumped into me when I entered the bar, and I felt his hand in my pocket."

Nina suddenly felt cold and began to shiver involuntarily. The pen drives. What on earth had she taken on?

"Did Prof. Menon meet you in the bar?"

"No, just before."

Delving for his pants, Roy quickly began rummaging through the pockets.

"They are with me… the pen drives. But why the secret pocket?" asked Nina.

Roy groaned," Self-defence. Amma."

"Amma?"

"Her habit of going through my pockets, Nina."

Roy was looking at Nina, the grin slowly fading.

"What is it, Nina? Why did that man search my pocket?"

Nina felt ashamed for not having confided in Maya chechi and Roy. They had the right to know. Her silence had endangered them.

Feeling deeply ashamed, she said, "Come for lunch, Roy. Maya chechi is waiting. I am sorry to have kept things to myself."

Smiling ruefully, she added, "Your secret pockets and my silence are both responses to our hovering mothers."

Roy was silent as she continued. He listened to her patiently, without interruption. When she spoke about the intruder in the sarpakava, he laughed. Nina, who was close to tears, looked at him sharply.

"I pity the man who dares to arouse her wrath. Let's not mention anything to her yet. The theft of the fish has upset her enough, and she will now grow anxious about you, if she thinks you are in danger… of being accosted, or attacked? You might as well have brought your mother along."

Nina was quiet for a moment.

Then she said, "But if my presence spells trouble. I will go."

"What will it solve?" asked Roy. "If trouble followed you here, it will follow you back again. Nope, don't go back yet. Mystery lingers in the pen drives. Nina, you have unwittingly, perhaps, set something into motion." He paused. "I am, frankly, curious. Let me help."

Nina nodded her assent. She would read the transcripts first.

PART - 2

We shall not cease from exploration

And the end of all our exploring

Will be to arrive where we started

And know the place for the first time.

Through the unknown, remembered gate

When the last of earth left to discover

Is that which was the beginning;

—T.S. Eliot, from "Little Gidding,"
Four Quartets.

Chapter VII

"O Captain! My Captain!"

Diary of Damon Zia, son of Onasis Pavlidis and captain of the ship Triton.

18 July 1889

We reached Muziris with the fair wind, Hippalus, blowing on the sixth of May and made haste to the small town of Cranganore. Here, we were told by the natives that the thampuran, who is the lord of the place, wanted to see me. I have been coming to Muziris, and know the language of the place, Malayalam, well. There was an old sailor and interpreter who has taught it to me, over the many travels to Muziris and back. The natives of Muziris are dark-skinned, small-built, and sinewy. The majority have curly hair and, a few men of the upper caste wear it tied in a prominent bun, worn to one side of the head.

20 July 1889

The tharavadu, which is what the locals call the house in which the thampuran lives, is a sprawling building couched in the middle of an expanse of verdant green. The floors are a shiny black, and the doors have intricate designs wrought on them. The ceiling of polished teak captures and holds the light of the sun filtering in through the open windows. I sat watching the dust motes dance as I awaited the thampuran. I must have fallen asleep and awoke suddenly to a gentle breeze wafting from a handheld fan. A man was fanning me with a palm leaf, hand fan while another was seated on the large, gilded rosewood chair, across the room. The thampuran as it turned out had been waiting for me to wake up. The ministration by the man, Ramachandran, was a civilized attempt to bring me back to my surroundings. The thampuran is a slight, middle-aged man with a craggy face, scarred by smallpox. I looked at him and found his gaze boring into me as if to discover something. The man's entire strength was concentrated in the intensity of his gaze. When I looked up again, he was smiling. He gestured to me, to help myself to the banana chips and tea Ramachandran had placed near me. Sipping the frothy, lukewarm, milky tea we finalized the deal. He wanted a monopoly in trade. All of our ship's cargo. In exchange, we would have access to the finest spices produced in his estate. It took all of my newly acquired language skills and patient cajoling, to allow him to let me reserve a part of the cargo to purchase pearls, corals, ivory and semi-precious stones. He reluctantly agreed to let me retain a part of my cargo. He said he was certain he could procure the pearls. His divers would do that. The merchants he knew would supply the rest. He would make sure that I got the best deal. Not wanting to express my reservations, I nodded my approval for the thampuran is a powerful man. As an ally, he will be an asset. He offered me the lodge adjoining the tharavadu on the condition that only

I would live there. The crew could stay in the cottages that the thampuran owned, just outside of town.

4 August 1889

Somewhere in the middle of the night, the rain ceased its furious drumming on the roof. The cacophony has died. All that remains is the steady drip from the eves and the squelching sound of someone approaching the door. I gaze at the pale sunlight streaked with dust motes pouring in through windows placed high on the wall, documenting my impressions for lack of anything else to do. Soon, the room will be suffused by a pale, emerald green, a far cry from the fierce sun of the open sea. The pallid beauty has begun to wane on me, and I long to be back under the open sky. I must pause writing to fling open the door.

It was the thampuran's man, Ramachandran. He has brought a basket, covered with a banana leaf. My breakfast has, unfortunately, arrived. Boiled tapioca root accompanied by fish in rich gravy.

It is already well past the time for departure. The crew are getting restive. There was a brawl last night at the local arrack shanty involving one of the sailors. If we sail now, we will make it back to Piraeus before summer ends. The thampuran wants exclusivity in trade and has been a most commendable host. However, the transaction has slowed. The thampuran, unfortunately, has lost his wife to a snake bite. Or so they say. The locals talk, uninhibited by the presence of a videsi. They think I make no sense of the muttering and whispers, which surround me, as

I wander through the vast estate. She was ailing, or wasn't she? Poisoned? Some said she was killed by his sister who could command strange creatures to do her will. The air around the 'Nallukettu Tharavadu' is murky with rumours. Nallukettu refers to the architectural style of the house. Four blocks are constructed around a central courtyard open to the sky, allowing the large, matrilineal families of the Nair household to enjoy privacy while having access to the commonly owned property and facilities of the tharavadu house.

5 August 1889

Something strange has occurred to stir me out of the ennui which has been weighing my senses. Isolation and my sense of helplessness were smothering me like a grey cloud. My head was heavy as I made my way out into the thickly forested area at the back of the house. The red soil was rich and verdant. A luxurious plush carpet of green grew as far as my eyes could see. I made my silent way through the canopy of coconut palms to the clearing beyond. I was just about to step into the clear pool of light, but stopped, suddenly breathless. A girl stood under the parijat tree. She was reaching up to pluck the blooms which had not scattered in the morning deluge. Her breasts were bare, the nipples brownish-red and erect in the cool breeze. Her skin was the colour of ripened corn, her tresses hung to the ground in undulating waves. I remembered the stories of tree nymphs and would have quietly withdrawn, to watch from a distance, when she swung around. With a gasp, she dropped the blossoms she had gathered at the end of her mundu, the loincloth, and draped her hair around herself like a shawl. Momentarily, forgetting where I was, I moved towards her, but she was too quick. I got a glimpse of a face I will never forget.

Tracing my way back to the guest house, my mind kept going back to the encounter with the tree nymph. The old tharavadu house held many tales which will never be revealed to the world. But it will regale me through the long hours of waiting that hang upon me like fetters, I cannot break. I wonder if I can force an audience with the thampuran. The Triton, the trade ship that I captain, is driven by the Hippalus, the southwestern wind. The crew clamour to return before it dies. They want to be back to celebrate the festival of Dionysia held in the second half of December and the first half of January. The festival straddles the winter solstice and celebrates the cultivation of vines. Many of the sailors are from Attica, where the festival extends over several days. Some of them are also actors in travelling companies.

Lest this diary should fall in the hands of another, let it be known that I, Damon Zia, am the fourth son of Onasis Pavlidis, whose ships bore wine, gold coins, peridot, copper and textiles to the east in exchange for spice, silk and ivory. We have been trading with Muziris for six monsoons because it has the best pepper, semi-precious stones, pearls, sapphires, diamonds and ivory. Some ships also carry back with them dry coconut kernels which the women of Greece used for making skin care products.

I have learnt Malayalam from a local, who has served aboard the many ships which travel the silk route to Muziras. I am the Captain and the first man aboard. Most ships appoint local men, but I am both the negotiator and interpreter.

Well-versed in local traditions, I am aware that it is the convention for women to bare their breasts before a social superior. I have seen bare-breasted women of all ages working in the paddy fields adjoining the thampuran's vast estate. Some work in the kitchen, and it is so familiar a sight that I am no more startled into instinctively lowering my eyes. A breast tax is levied and paid by those who choose to do otherwise. There has been public shaming of women who have dared challenge the norm. I have warned my crew against ogling at the bare torsos of women. In Greece, women wear long, flowing garments which cover every inch of their skin. Even their feet are not visible under the ropes which swathe their feet. My men regard the natives as barbaric. But, the sight of a woman's uncovered body surges through their manhood. They have been away from their homes for many months. The locals do not communicate except for trade. Any errant behaviour by one of my crew would lead to their expulsion from a very rich source of revenue. I have to stop thinking of the lovely woman under the tree. It is madness to chase after an image. This curiosity is unnatural and yet, I must know who she is. My conversations with Ramchandran are always a source of much information, but the old family retainer is close-lipped when it comes to the thampuran and his family.

"Ramachandran," I called after the retreating man. He was returning from my cottage having found me absent.

"Yes, master. Is there something you need?"

"After the ample breakfast? The karimeen-curry was excellent. My compliments to the cook, and a small token of appreciation for you both."

I poured a few coins into the open, upturned palm and asked, "Any tree nymphs around here… a yakshi perhaps?"

Yakshis were women spirits, mostly benevolent protectors, found on carvings which decorated temples. They had to be appeased through prayer and offerings. Folklore depicted them as wandering spirits, beautiful women with long hair, who lured people to death.

Ramchandran's eyes widened with horror.

"Where did you see one?"

"Gathering flowers from the parijat tree."

Ramchandran doubled over with laughter, "That is koccha thampuratti."

"Koccha thampuratti?"

"The late thampuratti has been ill for years, and they do not have any progeny. After a sufficient period of mourning, the thampuran will marry the woman you saw. That is why we call her koccha thampuratti."

I thought of the ageing man with stubble covering his pock-marked face. Smallpox, I learnt, had raged through the town and none of the inhabitants of the old tharavadu had escaped. The thampuran's sister had remained unmarried. The iris of one of her eyes was clouded with a greyish-white circular spot. Though, there had been men ready to marry into such a powerful family, Janaki, the sister, had refused. I sometimes see her while walking across the huge ancestral property in which they live. A tall, statuesque figure, she had never looked up from the path she was walking, until the day a snake crossed, almost under her feet. I had halted, wary of the rustle in the grass. Then it emerged, a slim form, the coppery sheen on its back glistening as it made its unhasty way, across the track, into the foliage beyond. Janaki was looking at me, her head thrown back while her eyes engaged mine before she walked away. In that single moment, I sensed a presence, powerful and unsubdued.

With no access to the thampuran, I have decided to wait for a week before setting sail. I will have to forfeit a few supplies, but it is better to cut the losses than to reach after the other merchant ships have docked in the ports in Greece and begun the sale of their cargo.

6 August 1889

I made my way to the large green pond which lay at the extreme end of the thampuran's estate. I had been there before. Steps made of logs lead down to the cool green water, and I find it peaceful to sit there and let the tiny, silvery fish nibble at my toes. Just at the brink of descending, I stopped. Someone else was there before me. A woman dressed in the off-white settu mundu the locals wore, sat dipping her feet in the water. I would have withdrawn quietly, but she looked back, her eyes meeting mine unhesitatingly. With a wave, she indicated that I should come down. That face again, entrancingly beautiful. Instinct told me to walk away, but like a man in a dream from which I could not awaken, I drew closer till I was standing beside her.

She patted the space on the ground next to her and said, "Videshi, where are you from?"

"Greece," I replied, gazing at the upturned face.

Pointing to the holes along the sandy banks of the pond, from which a sudden flash of electric blue and copper flew out to merge with the foliage around, she asked, "Do you have these birds in your country?"

I could not help but nod as I lowered myself and sat alongside her.

"Like me, these kingfishers will always live beside the pond. They will never see Greece."

Her head was bent as she chewed on a stalk of grass.

"Not all birds are the same, you know. Some migrate to other places, far away, in search of sustenance."

"Like you?", she asked.

"Like me, for a season."

We sat in quiet companionship, lulled by the gently rippling water. I looked at her slender hands tipped with henna. I gritted my teeth. It felt so natural to reach out and hold it in my own.

I could not, however, stop myself from asking, "Are you shortly going to marry the thampuran… koccha thampuratti?"

The silence lengthened, merging with the growing shadows.

She suddenly looked up. Her eyes seared mine as she asked, "Will you marry me and take me with you to Greece?"

I was startled. "I am a sailor; we sail soon for Greece."

That reply was instantaneous, and I felt ashamed even as I uttered it. What a coward she must think of me.

"Like the migratory birds… at least stay the season," she appealed. Her eyes clung to mine, dissolving any resolve I might have had.

"I do not know your name, but I have no thoughts except about you since I first saw you under the parijat tree. If I marry you, it will not be for a season. Don't, you want to be the thampuratti?"

"I came to meet you here. I, I…" her voice trailed off.

I took her trembling hands and held them steady.

"Say it, I pleaded."

"It is you I want. No one else."

She told me that her name was Radha. She had seen me, many weeks ago, at the local shandy market and heard that I was a guest of the thampuran. When they invited her over to stay as a companion to his sister, she was not told that she would have to marry the thampuran. She had come in the hope of catching sight of me. For many days she had been wandering around the grounds, near the guest house, where she knew I was staying.

I felt, rather than saw, someone watching us. At the very edge of the cliff, just out of sight, stood a woman. Tall and erect, she was looking at us. She was too far off for me to see her expression, but I could recognize the stance. It was the thampuran's sister. She waved imperatively at me to come.

Radha moved fast, skipping over the logs in her haste to reach the observer. She reached her at a half sprint. I could see her beseeching the woman before she disappeared into the coconut grove. I quickened my pace, leaping over a coconut tree that had collapsed and lay sprawled, a trap for unwary strollers. The imperious figure stood still, the head held at an angle, watching me with unwavering eyes.

Her command was unambiguous. Behave or leave. I was equally adamant. I would marry Radha with the thampuran's permission. I would exchange the whole stock of the ship for her. I would honourably marry her according to the rites of the community. Determined though I was to do whatever it took to protect and claim Radha, I was totally unprepared for what came next.

"You can gladly have her if one of your crew marries me."

Seeing the shock writ large on my face, she continued, "A marriage only in name. He can leave with the ship."

"But, why?"

"That is not for you to ask." Her face was flushed. Her hands automatically went to her stomach.

In that moment, I knew. Her desperation stared at me from her eyes.

She was no longer young, though she still possessed a comely form. But who had dared to mate with her was the thought that sprang to my mind.

I looked away in embarrassment. When I looked up again, she repeated the gesture. Her eyes met mine, the desperation replaced by ferocity which challenged whatever expression must have flitted over my face. She averted her face so that I could not see her damaged eye. I realized how lissome she must have been before the disease ravaged her face. Before I could respond, she turned on her heels and left.

Her voice wafted back to me, "a hundred gold coins for the man who marries me."

It was mid-noon by now, and the sun blazed furiously down. Not a leaf stirred; the storm would break soon.

7 August 1989

I did not sleep until the early hours of the morning. I am a seaman. The sea beckons me, and to set sail into the unknown had always lured me more than any woman. My father had wanted me to marry early, and marry well.

There was no dearth of families which sought an alliance with ours, but I had unhesitatingly turned down the best. Now, I am like a man enchanted by the sirens. I cannot leave until I make her mine. I will never leave until she is beside me. Not for a season, but till we reach the tunnel of eternity.

I will ask Markos, my second in command, whether he would marry Janaki. As it has been for me, the sea is the only mistress Markos knows. But Markos is not frugal. He lives the good life like all sailors do when they reach land. A hundred gold coins for a sham? It would not be hard to convince him to play the role. I smiled as I thought of the travelling actors on board. There were at least a dozen who could be persuaded and would be more than willing to play the role. But they all drank the local brew, and a tipsy sailor loves nothing better than telling a tale. Markos drank only the wine which had lain buried deep, for years, in the soil of Greece. The sailors knew the wine they had brought was a commodity for trade. For them, to consume it was sacrilegious. Forbidden, under all circumstances, it was regarded as a wilful act of self-destruction and punishable under the rules which governed the sea trading community.

8 August 1889

Markos arrived in response to my summons. For a brief moment, the room turned dark as he stood at the door, peering into the room through eyes permanently screwed against the blazing sun at sea. He ducked, his large frame scrapping the sides of the doorway as he swaggered in. He stood, his legs wide apart as if the floor would begin rocking under him. Would this free-spirited seaman take the bait? It was over faster than I thought. His laughter threatened to rip the roof off the building as he nodded his acceptance. As a travelling actor, he made love to men dressed as women he explained as he attempted to rise from the floor, where he had flopped with helpless laughter. For a hundred gold coins, he would marry a coconut tree, and ask no questions.

Ramchandran ushered me into the presence of the thampuran's sister. The room was at the back of the house, and I had to walk past several portraits of men and women, whose expressions were fortunately hidden by the gloom. I felt like I had entered Hades, where spirits of dead people floated around me. Janaki was seated on a swing and sat facing the door.

"Yes," her voice rang out peremptorily.

Momentarily, blinded by the light pouring in from tall, narrow windows which punctuated the walls, I lifted my hands to shield my eyes. Dazzled by emerging from the dark corridor into the blinding light, I failed to see the slim form which sat on the other side of the swing. Radha. She was gazing at me with such intensity that when our eyes met, all else swam out of focus. The room blurred, and all I could hear above the ticking of my heart was a clock chiming the hour, somewhere in the vastness of the house.

"What brings you here?" asked the woman on the swing.

I realized that the thampuran's sister had employed a well-known strategy. One used in war to take the foe by surprise. The room to which I had been summoned, and Radha's unexpected presence, at an event which demanded confidentiality, were calculated to destroy my defences.

"My second in command, Marcos is willing," I said meeting her unflinching stare.

"When?"

"As soon as you want the marriage."

I was enraged, as any man in my circumstance would be. I strove to keep my voice steady and continued to gaze down at her.

"In a week. I will ask our family astrologer for an auspicious timing for the ceremony."

"And Radha?"

I hated to make it sound like a barter.

"Your sambandam will take place on the same day."

She looked away, but not before I caught an expression halfway between a smirk and smug amusement on her face. The cat had caught its mice. Radha, I dared not look at again. I would not display any further emotion before the other woman.

11 August 1989

I have roamed the thampuran's estate night and day, but there is no sign of Radha. Where have they sent her? My heart is in turmoil. I want to march in and confront the thampuran and his sister. But I know, I will learn nothing. This waiting game is not for me.

Markos came just as I was preparing to go across and demand an audience with the thampuran. He persuaded me to come with him to the local arrack shop. There the workers from the tharavadu congregate, their day's labour done. We might learn something.

We joined the rest of the crew. No special attention was paid to us other than the replenishing of the pitcher of arrack, from which the men drank. Markos nudged me as two men approached, calling out over their shoulders for the local brew. They sat on the bench behind me. So close, that if I leaned back, I would bump them. I realized that they had deliberately chosen a space away from the other customers. Our presence did not matter. Videshi folk, they thought, would shield them from curious onlookers. They could talk uninterrupted and without being overheard. As their tongues loosened, I learnt that an astrologer had been called and consulted. There were rumours that the thampuran's sister had consented to marry so that the family lineage could continue. The astrologer was being consulted for an auspicious day. It was likely to be soon. The cloth merchant had been sent for. The priest would perform the 'punyaham', a purification ceremony, on the very next day following the mourning period. One of the men cursed the thampuran, calling him a sister fucker. The other gave a loud guffaw which was quickly stifled.

12 August 1989

The sambandam ceremony is tomorrow. Markos was called late, last night, and given a pair of settu mundu to be presented to Janaki, at an auspicious time, after dawn. He went there as instructed and set his eyes on her for the first time She surveyed him carefully and then dismissed him with a wave of her hand. Just as my agitation was reaching its peak, Ramachandran came with a pair of gold-laced mundus, wrapped in a length of silk cloth.

"For Radha," he said.

Was the man aggrieved? I couldn't tell. His face was bland and expressionless as ever.

I was so relieved that I slumped on the bed. The thampuran's sister had been as good as her word.

14 August 1989

Much has happened. Radha is mine to hold and caress while the blood runs through my veins.

The ceremony which solemnized our union was simple to the point of being absurd. We exchanged garlands, and I gave her the mundus. A similar ceremony had served to formalize the arrangement between Janaki and Markos. I had something for her though, the caduceus. It has been in our family for generations and is the most precious object I possess. The caduceus has cleared the way for me in many of my voyages. The value lies not in the jewels that are embedded in it, which are undoubtedly precious, but in the caduceus being a protective element. It is a symbol of kinship recognized by sailors, maritime traders and thieves. No ship that I have captained has ever been attacked by pirates. The word has spread that I am in possession of the caduceus. That has like an invisible armour saved me from being robbed and killed by those who fear its power, even while not believing in the spirit of unity it represents. The mantle of protection in which the caduceus wraps those who possess it is known across the seas. Those, who would sail against the wind know they will be pursued and skewered to death if they perpetuated harm against one protected by the caduceus. It is this jewel that I have gifted Radha. May it protect the generations to come as it has me.

On the night following the nuptials, Radha was ushered into my room by a giggling bevvy of women. An old, toothless woman swayed her hips in mock seduction, her betel-stained, cavernous mouth widening in obscene laughter. I felt myself flushing as I moved my gaze away. After propping Radha against the pillows, they left singing a song which I found hard to understand. The sound was raucous. Their departure left the room oddly still. It was like the world had shrunk into the small figure reclining against the pillows. She suddenly sprang out of bed and spreading a mat on the floor, lay down. I lay alongside her and she stared back at me. The demure look with eyes downcast had been replaced by one I could not quite decipher till she burst into laughter, eyes bright with mischief.

Snuggling up to me she announced, "I am theendari."

Seeing me blink, she explained that it was that time of the month when she was considered impure because she was menstruating. She had kept that a secret because our nuptials would be delayed. In Kerala, during the time a woman was considered theendari, she was banished to a secluded space in the dark interiors of the home. In most tharavadu homes there was a small, often windowless room to which women withdrew when they were menstruating, or during the post-natal phase. I found the idea reprehensible, and carried Radha, protesting, to bed. The day's events had made me exhausted, and I soon drifted into sleep listening to Radha snore softly against my chest.

22 August 1989

The rain has been ceaseless. Sheets of rain cascade down holding us virtual prisoners. Ramachandran braves the rain bringing us victuals and drinks. Radha darts out like the garden nymph I mistook her for and returns looking flushed and seductive. I have possessed her again and yet again, but it is never enough. Her silken flanks open to receive me, her stomach taut under my marauding hands as my mouth moves to nipples that taste of the rain. She shudders, and as I move back to gaze at her face, draws my head down, cleaving to me. Radha moulds herself to me as we make discoveries in an act which is as instinctive as our mingled breaths.

Today, as we lay intertwined, the door suddenly caved in. Markos nearly walked in on us today. The door was held shut and latched by a mere hook.

I had forgotten to padlock it by raising the wooden bar and securing it. Markos opened the front door with a shove of his hand, the latch giving away under the onslaught of man and muscle. Radha jumped out and raced away, clutching the sheet to her chin. Walking naked to the door, I shoved him out with a terse command to wait. The expression on his face was indescribable. Embarrassed and confused, he muttered an apology when I joined him outside, after donning my clothes. He would set sail immediately. There was no need to linger. I was to meet the thampuran to receive the payment and finalise the goods that we would be taking back with us.

Markos looked visibly distraught. I called over my shoulders to Radha to let her know I would be back soon and led Markos to the seat of rough-hewn boulders under a canopy nearby. Barely had he seated himself that Markos began speaking and gesticulating wildly. The profanities he uttered cannot be produced here. It is best that they should vanish forever into the murky stillness of the afternoon. There would be a storm soon, I could smell its approach.

The she-devil had emasculated him. She was a Gorgon; any man would turn into stone at the sight of her. Hearing me protesting faintly, he burst into vehement speech.

"Did you know she has a white cast in one eye?"

I nodded, "Didn't YOU?"

"That is the mark of the devil. Her face is covered with pits which burn like hellfires."

"You saw her. She did not cheat you," I reprimanded Markos.

"And let's not forget you married her for a bagful of gold coins."

Markos continued to look aggrieved. She had forced him to consummate the marriage which he had been more than willing to, knowing his duties as a husband. It was the racket she made in the throes of orgasm which had incapacitated him. It sounded like the copulation of cats.

This had gone on for a couple of days, but this morning he had been summoned to the presence of thampuran. He was given orders to leave within the week. Of the thampuran's sister, there was no sign. I let Markos ramble on till he grew silent. I have no remorse. He has made a bargain and must keep it, be it with the very devil himself.

I saw the now familiar figure of Ramachandran approaching from a distance. I waited knowing that he was bearing a missive from the tharavadu house. The letter was addressed to me.

The letter was a formal acceptance of all our terms of trade. The terms were very generous. I was to have complete and sole access to the spices that grew on the thampuran's estate with the promise of ivory and pearls to be procured by the thampuran's men, his divers and hunters, in exchange for wine, gold and the fine linen we had brought from Greece. The ship was to be laden with cargo, and we were to leave before the week was over. Markos would go, but there was no way I could leave Radha. A time may come when I have to briefly return to Greece but not without Radha. She would come. How would she not?

1 November 1989

The Triton has set sail with Markos as its captain. I had a short meeting with the thampuran, to inform him about my plan to travel to Kasi and beg his indulgence for my absence. I am leaving for the city of Kasi to buy silks, which are much in demand among the upper echelon of Greek society. I will go when the cold sets in the north of this vast country. It will be a change from this warm, tropical climate. The thampuran did not demur. Kasi silk is famous for its exquisite sheen and the feel of the material. The thampuran would like me to procure sarees for the members of his family. He said his sister would exult in possessing the precious silk worn by the Travancore royal family and that she would look aristocratic. I agreed. Markos might not have. But Markos is well on his way, the reward of gold coins stowed safely in his bag. The thampuran's sister has an alibi for the baby growing in her belly, and Radha, my love is safely by my side. A fortuitous trade for all concerned.

If only I could take Radha with me! But it will be a long, arduous journey and she is with a child.

4 November 1989

I have left Radha at her mother's place. Our baby will arrive when the Triton docks at Muziris again. I am on my way to Kasi, travelling part of the way by canoe, horseback and bullock cart. It will take me three weeks to get there. The thampuran has sent armed men as escorts.

The route is safe except for dacoits who live among the hills. These men will not take me hostage. I have with me purses of gold coin which will smooth my way. There is honour among the thieves yet. The caduceus will not serve me here as it has on the high sea, where it paved a way even through the most dreaded of pirates and brigands which the sea harbours. That, I will leave with Radha; it is an amulet and may it serve her well.

The diary came to an end with the last entry. Nina scrolled down and back again. It was over. There was nothing more. Had Damon Zia returned from Benaras and seen his child?

Nani Kutty, Radha's daughter with her light skin and hazel eyes had been a celebrated beauty of her times. The woman, she resembled, had only one sambandam, given birth to seven children and died in ripe, old age. Did she have siblings, wondered Nina, an only child herself. So much was shrouded in the mists of time. Would she be able to reach back over the years to know a past which had cast its long shadows on her present?

She mulled over what she had learnt. Possessing a caduceus was of importance to the seaman, and yet he had bequeathed it as an amulet. Even at the moment of being passionately in love, the possibility of separation had occurred to him. He had wanted to protect Radha in the event of his absence. The caduceus was a powerful symbol, and the pendant had value beyond the jewel-embedded, precious metal. Hidden out of sight, in lockers, the caduceus she possessed had disappeared from public view.

Her trip to Europe had changed it all. Someone had triggered the alarm leading to the chain of events which had brought her back, to the home of her ancestors, to discover her roots. The more she dug, the darker it got. She seemed to have entered a tunnel from where there was no turning back. Even if she were to keep it buried in bank vaults, the caduceus had made her a marked woman. Her best defence lay in knowing the truth. She sighed. It had grown dark, and the house was asleep along with its inhabitants. The ancient dwelling of her ancestors made strange noises as it sank into slumber. She heard it gasp as if awakening from a nightmare, and then all was still again. The hollow sound, "chonk,chonk,chonk" like someone was knocking, was from a nightjar. It sounded close at hand ending in a squawk as something disturbed it. Nina crept into bed beside Maya chechi as she would do when she was a little girl. The darkness outside seemed to be teeming with the spirits of dead people.

Chapter VIII

Radha's Confession

Nina was unable to read the second piece of writing which had been digitised. She begged Maya chechi to join her. It was in Malayalam.

Maya chechi ran her eyes over it and said, "There are no dates on this, Nina. Ammini Amma or Radha as she liked to call herself, wrote to vent. It is fragmented like the sobs that accompany grieving"

Maya chechi began to read, her voice bringing alive the emotional outbursts of a woman from a century ago.

Damos, my Damos is back from travel. He has bought the most beautiful silks to send to Greece when the ship returns to Muziris. He has bought some for me as well. What will I do with them? I only wear our mundu. Maybe a blouse or two to make Damos happy? Why is he not happy? He has a strange, faraway look in his eyes, and he seems to be searching the horizon with his sailor's eyes.

The ship, Markos captains, docked on the same day, as the one, on which I went into labour. Damos did not want to leave my side, but the midwife sent him away. The birthing room is no place for men, she said. They will grow faint, or cause a commotion if the labour is hard. My labour was long and unendurable. Just when I thought I had pushed with the last remaining strength, the baby came out with a whoosh. But the midwife said there was one more baby to follow. I wanted to leave my body and go away to a safe place. Far away from the blood and the screams. Were they mine? I felt the midwife splash my face with water. I could not return. My soul had fled far away. It was then that she reached in to pull out another infant. I heard it cry as I burrowed into a deep, dark hole.

....

Damos is jubilant. He has two sons who look just like him. The same colouring and thick, tawny hair, their eyes the colour of the sea. They have nothing of me. I have named them Appu and Kuttan. At least, their names will reflect their origin.

....

Damos does not write anymore. He said he was recording our lives together, so as never to forget why a Greek had chosen to live in Muziris. I dare not ask him why he writes no more. He gets provoked by everything and nothing. Then he goes away to the seashore to gaze out at the sea. He takes the boys with him, and I insist on Ramachandran accompanying them. I am afraid the sea will claim them as her own, just the way she has my husband, my Damos.

....

Damos has changed from the man who cherished me, making me feel like he could never have enough of me. He still wants me physically, but now, it is as if to blot out the demons raging within him. He attacks me, making furious love, deaf to my involuntary cries of pain. I am not the same after the boys were born. I am broken, but he does not give me time to heal. I bleed and am bruised. If I hold back, what will I have of Damos, the Damos I love? The only time he holds me in his arms is in the throes of the violence he perpetuates on me. At other times, his eyes rest on me briefly before he goes to satiate himself with the sight of the sea.

The thampuran called me to the tharvadu house, yesterday. He wants to call a priest to perform vidhyarambham, the ritual to initiate a child into literacy before education begins, for Appu and Kuttan. The ceremony will take place for my boys as well as his sister's son. The child is the thampuran's own, and no one believes it to be Markos's son. The child has a large head which shakes with palsy. My heart breaks to see him watch as my two robust boys run and tumble about. I must remove the drishti, the evil eye, that I unwittingly cast on my sons. They say a mother's drishti hurts her children the most. I must ask someone how to do it. I remember my mother taking salt, red chili pods, mustard seeds and other things to throw into the fire. I will wave it around the boys three times after sunset and then walk away to burn any ill effects of my pride, my love for them. Oh! Why am I so fearful? It is as if a cold, clammy hand clutches my heart amid the joy I take in them… my adorable sons.

. . . .

The vidyarambham was conducted with all three boys sitting in a row. The boys wrote 'Hari Shree Ganapate' on layers of uncooked rice grains, spread out on silver plates, and took the blessings of the priest. The thampuran gave the dakshina which included several gold coins, fruits, and other kinds of produce to the priest on our behalf.

His sister is not happy about the thampuran's kindness to my boys. She fears for her sons. My son will have as much right to inherit the title and the tharavadu house as her son. Like all the women in the family, I am entitled to protection and the family name.

. . . .

I have not had my period for forty-five days. I know I am pregnant. Damos has not come to my bed since the last time the sheets turned crimson with my blood. He was shocked and for the first time in a long while looked at me with concern. Or was it repugnance? The nightly battering has stopped. I do not know whether to grieve or exult in my freedom.

The ship from Greece owned by Damos has docked in Kochi, instead of Cranganore. Damos has gone there to meet the crew. The port there is bigger and for a while now, trade has moved from here to Kochi. The thampuran will not be happy with the change of route.

. . . .

Damos is leaving for his home. Markos brought a letter written by a man who, by rights, is my father-in-law. The word seems strange even in writing. He wants nothing from me but longs to see Damos and his grandsons, my sons. Does he not realise that he is asking for my soul? Damos cradles me with the same gentleness that I knew before. He will leave and take the boys with him. I must let them go. I fear Janaki. I see resentment growing in her eyes. The evil witch, the thampuran's sister, may lay a spell on them. They will be safer with their father than with me.

Ommana chechi pulled the gold waistband tightly over my stomach. It barely encircled my waist. I looked away, so as not to meet her knowing look. The nausea has subsided, but the pain in my side refuses to go away even though I have rubbed it with the salve the vaidyan gave. The area is red and scabbed like that place deep inside me ever since Damos left with Appu and Kuttan. It will never be whole again. My little boys. Damos in miniatures. Damos wants to introduce them to his family. They have inherited his looks and are claimants to a huge shipping empire. What can I give them except the yearning of my heart? It is six years since Damos met his family. Three months since he left. He would have stayed if he had known... He would have been alive. Like the boys. They live and thrive, heirs to what Damos had spurned when he chose to return by the next ship. Markos says the storm was a fiend which wrecked the ship. All men escaped. Damos was the last to clamber into the little, rescue boat, but before they could heave him in, the swirling current created by the sinking ship tugged him away and carried him along. For long did Markos and his men strive to move in the direction that his bobbing head was last seen, but a fiend held them tight. Was it a yakshi who died before she knew such happiness as was mine? The thampuran's first wife? Everyone knows that it was his sister who warmed his bed. The thampuratti's marital bed was cold. The curse of the thampuratti has fallen on the house of the thampuran. The thampuran was found on the same bed, where he had lain with his sister, cold as a corpse and frothing at the mouth. It would have been better if he had died. But who would have married me then? I am pregnant. This child is mine. Damos took his. The thampuran will let me bring it up as his own. His own child, Unni, born of his sister has a head larger than the biggest pumpkin, I have set my eyes on, and it shakes with palsy. Accursed indeed is this place and yet, I am the thampuran's new bride. His sister, or shall I call her his woman, bedecked me with her own hands. She of implacable will. Grim and greying, no more can she warm up her brother's frozen groin. But she labours on to ensure the continuation of the tharavadu. My child will ensure that. If a girl, the lineage and if a boy, the future thampuran and karnavar. The thampuran is a descendant of the royal family. His father had sambandam with a Nair woman and as her eldest son, he is the head and subsequently, his son will be.

．．．．．．．．．．．．．．．．．．．．．．．．．．．．．．．．．

My little one is three months old. She looks like Damos. All my children do. Her eyes, her beautiful, square-tipped fingers, the mop of golden curls. My golden girl. My Damos.

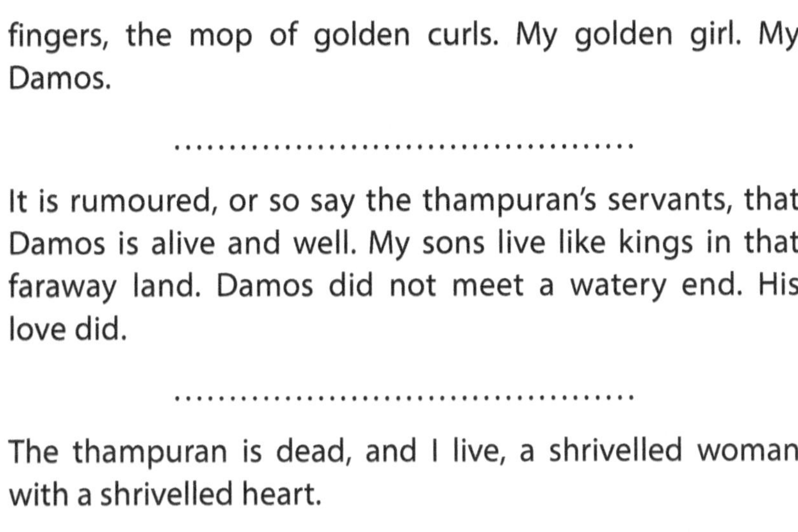

It is rumoured, or so say the thampuran's servants, that Damos is alive and well. My sons live like kings in that faraway land. Damos did not meet a watery end. His love did.

The thampuran is dead, and I live, a shrivelled woman with a shrivelled heart.

Radha's journal ended on the anguished cry of a wounded creature.

Nina swallowed hard. The lump in her throat hurt as she blinked to hold back her tears. How had Radha lived out the rest of her life? Had she kept the journal going? There were a few mangled bits of palm leaves, remains of scripts from the past, eaten by white ants and time. Radha's story would live on, coloured by the imagination of those who had known her until time extinguished even those memories.

Chapter IX

A Mid Wife's Tale

Maya was pleased with the discovery that a Greek, Damon Zia, was their ancestor. Having lived all her life in Kodungallur, and travelled very little, she was at a stage in life where the 'what-ifs' no more plagued her. What remained was a pride in the land of her forefathers. As for the world, it arrived at her door, every morning, amidst the folds of a pleasingly crackling newspaper which she perused, tea in hand.

Radha's outpourings haunted her. Reading her short, anecdotal account of her life with Damos was oddly disturbing. Damos had satiated himself and then moved on, thought Maya, taking with his sons as trophies. Ammini Amma had been left with nothing but a wounded womb. She sat down to read once again the confessional journals of Damos and Radha and lost herself in the annals of the past. There were no pictures or portraits of Ammini Amma or Radha as she had called herself. She must have had that rare, elusive beauty which Nina possessed to have held Damon Zia captive, until an unforeseen circumstance separated them. Like Nina, she wondered how Ammini Amma had come to marry again. She had married the thampuran, their ancestor on her mother's side. The couple did not have any progeny. Nanikutty, the famed beauty, had been her only child.

So, Muziris had been Kodungallur after all. Maya had read enough scholastic debate about the plausible location of Muziris to realise that Damon Zia's diary was of historic importance. But the diary was too deeply personal to be shared with the world. Muziris, Maya mused was the spice garden which had brought the Christians, Muslims and Jews to the erstwhile town of Cranganore, later renamed Kodungallur. Though the remnants of Jewish dwellings existed in present-day Kodungallur, the majority had left after they were attacked by Arab traders. They had been given shelter in Cochin by the Raja of Travancore and had been permitted to build a synagogue there. The Jewish town still existed with very few families, most of the Jews having migrated to Israel. Maya's musings were brought short by a gentle squeeze on her shoulder. Nina stood with two cups of tea, delicately balanced, in her free hand.

Knowing Maya's addiction to tea, she had brewed a fresh cup for her.

Without a preamble, Nina began, "Let us visit Kartyayani Amma."

Maya nodded. "I was planning on visiting Leela. She is a distant cousin. But you know that?"

"No, I didn't. I met her that day for the first time. She seems to have known Nani Kutty."

"Kartyayani Amma is not always coherent. There are times when she is completely lucid. She remembers many things from her childhood though she cannot remember her own name at times. Let us go, this afternoon."

Nina shortened her stride as she walked alongside Maya chechi. They were passing through a narrow lane with fences, made of woven coconut leaves, on either side. Maya chechi skirted around a small pond, green with algae, beyond which lay a tiny, thatched cottage. The door was ajar. Leela sat at the doorway combing her long, oiled hair with her fingers. Hearing them approach, she hastily wound her hair into a knot and offered them water to wash their feet. Nina was impressed with the inside of the house. It was scrupulously clean, the floor scoured and polished till it gleamed in the sunlight which had followed them in. Leela spread a mat on which Nina plonked down instantly. Maya lowered herself with some effort, supporting herself against the wall. Leela hastened to fetch a chair from the inner room with Nina following her.

Where was Kartyayani Amma? Nina looked around. Just as she was about to turn back, she paused. She was startled to see what she thought was a pile of clothes, sit up, and beckon her.

"Nani Kutty, have you come to see me? And brought your youngest child with you? She is alive because of me. Both of you nearly died at that time. Your eighth child. All born alive… alive."

Nina sat near her, holding her hand, her back turned to the window.

Looking down at their interlocked fingers, Kartyayani Amma said," Did you go out in the sun, your skin has become as dark as mine. You don't look like a videshi anymore."

Nina pressed her hands gently.

Kartyayani Amma continued, "Both are dead. Both paid for their sins. My mother and Janaki, the thampuran's sister."

Gazing past Nina, as the ghosts of the past came alive before her, Kartyayani Amma added, "My mother took Radha's child, your only brother and put the stillborn child in its place. Shiv-Shiva, Shiv-Shiva. May not the sins of the mother be visited on the daughter. That she-devil forced her to. Janaki." She spat loudly into the corner of the room and waved her fingers agitatedly as if to force someone out of her sight.

"Your son born in incest will come to no good, Janaki," she yelled turning to look at the window as she drew closer to Nina and began to whimper.

Leela came rushing in hearing her mother's raised voice and stopped short when she saw Nina holding her close.

Kartyayani Amma looked up at her defiantly and said, "I will tell Nani Kutty the whole truth. She must find her brother. I will not be allowed to die till I confess. I am so tired; I want to rest."

Leela gesticulated towards the door. Nina gently disentangled the hands holding hers and got up to leave.

"Help me," Leela whispered fiercely. "Please let me calm her down."

She looked angry and distraught. Nina wondered whether she had been too intrusive. She had precipitated into the open, a secret, buried for years under resigned silence.

They sat in silence until Leela entered, bearing heaped plates of sweet flattened rice and pale, milky, lukewarm tea.

She looked at Nina and said, "Amma has hallucinations. Don't believe what she says."

Nina countered, "We have unearthed writing which gives credence to your mother's protestations."

Nina was bluffing. She had a hunch that Leela knew something that would throw light on the mystery which shrouded the caduceus. Nina wanted an explanation for the happenings that had sneaked up on her and threatened to cloud her present.

Leela looked startled and then quickly schooled her expression. She got up to pull the threadbare curtains against the western sun.

The pedestal fan, in the corner, barely made a dent in the uncomfortably warm room.

Maya chipped in, "Leela, we are family. Nina needs to know the truth. All of us may be endangered by your silence."

She quickly narrated the series of events which had occurred.

"At this point, we are fishing in the dark. Tell us all that you know."

Leela looked out at the darkness which had gathered outside the window. There was a distant roll of thunder and the sound of rain pattering on the roof. With a sigh, was it of defeat or relief, Nina could not tell, Leela began to speak. At first, she groped for words and would not meet their eye. Soon, her words were coming in rhythm with the torrential rain outside.

Much of what she knew was overheard from her grandmother and mother. Both had been dependent on the thampuran's household for sustenance. Some things had been witnessed by them; others were titbits of information gathered from the servants' quarters where they were housed for many years. Though related to the thampuran, they had worked as maids, cooks and midwives to those in residence in the tharavadu house.

Smallpox had devastated the town of Kodungallur, not sparing any home, not even the great house of the thampuran. Both the son and the daughter of the house had been ravaged by it. The young master was just twenty-one and his sister a mere sixteen. Kalyani Amma, her grandmother, who was then a child, used to take food to the room, in the attic, where the siblings lay in isolation. She had to place the plates at the threshold of the room, knock and then leave. One day, the room was ajar, and she heard the girl moan and call out aloud. Peering in to ascertain whether she needed to procure help, she witnessed the young master lying upon his sister, pounding her with his thighs as he gasped for breath. Kalyani knew what was happening. Children who grow up within the narrow confines of a little, shared room lose their innocence very early in life. For them, copulating humans are reminiscent of the dogs and cattle mating in the countryside. She padded down to her mother and whispered to her. A hand was clapped over her mouth, and she was dragged away, out of the earshot of others. There had been talk. Semen had been found on the mats when they were removed. Since no one entered the room, the young master would keep the used mats out before taking the fresh ones in. No one dared tell the thampuran, their father. But someone must have. The young mistress was removed from the attic and placed in a room, on the same floor as her parents. When her scabs dried and fell off, the iris of one of her eyes was partially covered by a dull film of white. She was accursed. The young master emerged from the effects of the epidemic, comparatively unscathed.

"Strange are the ways of God and men," commented Leela as she paused for breath.

For many years, the young mistress was away. No one dared ask where. Then she came back, imperious and cold. It was as if all the warmth and spontaneity which she had possessed, as a young girl, had been strangulated for good. The old thampuran had passed away and the young master, now married, had taken his place. The thampuratti was a young woman of impeccable lineage. Her family was aristocratic and could boast of connections with the royal family. She excelled at playing the veena, and the young master often joined her, their clear young voice ringing through the household. The servants smiled and went about their work with a sense of anticipation. Kalyani Amma, though still a child herself, hoped to assist her mother in bringing into the world a child of the tharavadu. Leela paused as if she did not want to go on. Maya laid a hand on her shoulder, shook her gently and nodded.

The servants were the first to notice that the thampuran came home very late. He let himself in after everyone else had gone to bed. As per his order, no one was to await his return. The thampuratti turned listless, and her voice no more rang joyously through the household. She began to fade while Janaki, the thampuran's sister glowed with a strange radiance. Disfigured and pockmarked, there was something undeniably mesmerising about her. Tongues began to wag, but people dismissed it as mere gossip based on conjecture.

The news must have travelled. The thampuratti's family members visited and were courteously received. They left, anxiety writ large on their faces, none the wiser for having come. The thampuratti was wasting away, but the many renowned physicians who came to treat her found nothing wrong with her. And so, she lived on as if holding on to life and refusing to surrender. Some said she was poisoned.

In the end, she suffered from delirium and was kept confined, alone except for a nurse. A gentlewoman, the sight of Janaki would send her into hysteria. As for the thampuran, he barely visited her. One day, she hid behind the door and threw a knife at him. It glanced off but, after that, all visits ceased. When she died, even before the mourning period was over, the thampuran's sister, Janaki, married a Greek sailor. He was one of the crew of a ship which did trade with the thampuran. He left within a few days of the wedding, but eight months later Janaki bore a son.

"He was not a premature baby, and was as dark as their sin," added Kartyayani Amma. She had crawled into the room on all fours while the others in the room were immersed in the recital. Leela moved her frail frame and cradled her in her arms as if she were a child.

Looking at Nina, Kartyayani Amma said, "How sunburned you have become, child. You were like the videshi when you were born. Your twin brother had his father's blue eyes. You had poocha kannu but grew beautiful like Ammini Amma. My mother was there at your birth. But she did a bad thing; she gave the boy to the Jewess."

"Which Jewess?" asked Nina. The story was getting more and more fantastic.

Chapter X

The Drowned Sailor Returns

There was a sudden clattering at the door. The room fell silent as all turned to look. Who could it be at this hour? The rain was coming down in swathes, and the drumming on the tin roof had risen to a crescendo. The sound of someone knocking loudly could be heard above the clamour of the rain. Nina was the first to recover. She called out. A man's voice answered, but it was drowned in a crash of thunder. Peering from the window, she saw the dark shape of a man, water pouring off him in streams. She banged at the glass to draw the attention of whoever was out there. In the dim light of the naked bulb, that someone had turned on, she recognised the pale contours of the man's face. Derek. Without another word, she threw open the door, and he entered, bending his head to avoid the low door beam. Kartyayani Amma began to shriek in hysteria, the saliva frothing at the corners of her mouth.

"The drowned sailor has returned to avenge his son," shrieked the ancient woman.

Nina saw that Maya chechi wore a stunned expression while Leela was cowering back, cradling her mother in her arms.

Realising that neither of them would recognise Derek, she said, "It is Derek, my husband."

Maya had not attended Nina's wedding. It had been a quiet affair at the registrar's office, and the photographs of the couple had come at a time when Maya was grieving her husband. They had been relegated to the growing pile, at the bottom of her cupboard, with scarcely a glance.

Derek shook himself as a dog might, spraying Nina with water. Leela had recovered enough to offer him a towel, and Maya moved hastily to summon Roy to their assistance.

Kartyayani Amma shook her head dolefully at Nina and said, "This is a sign, an omen. You must trace your own."

Unflustered by the apparent confusion he had created, Derek squatted on the mat and soon had them engrossed in his tales of living in the South Western Ghats montane rainforests. He told them that these forests were an ecoregion with a large number of elephants, tigers and several species. However, there were daily encroachments on their habitats through the conversion of forest land into coffee and tea estates. Derek spoke about the mushrooming of resorts and the destruction of forests to cater to ecotourism. This had to be halted. The government had sought the help of the local tribes in helping them to monitor and prevent further encroachments. Derek acted on an advisory board to the government, and he often arbitrated on their behalf with local farmer groups and committees.

One of the biggest issues was the conflict between farmers who lived along the borders of the forest and the elephants. Since unchecked encroachment had choked the elephant corridors, the elephants ventured deeper and deeper into estates attracted by ripening fruits and coffee berries. No one dared grow jackfruit on their estates any more. That was like a clarion call to elephants from miles around; the ripening fruit drew elephants like flies to honey. Venturing elephants were shot or electrocuted. Electric wiring was prohibited but had been put up surreptitiously. Derek shook his head. He preferred facing a tusker than having an irate farmer draw his gun on him. Nina clasped his hand and pressed it. She looked up at his face and felt her heart lurch. She moved so that she was sitting with her back pressed against his knees. She felt his warmth, it swirled around her. Kartyayani Amma had recovered and was looking at Derek earnestly. She propelled herself forward until she was crouching in front of them. She stared at Derek, her eyes alive with interest. She seemed to have understood something of what Derek had been narrating. She asked him whether he had heard of the great tusker which had rampaged through the town of Kodungallur, causing havoc and bringing life, in the town, to a standstill. When Derek shook his head and gesticulated for her to go on, she began to croon the song of Kavalappara, the temple elephant, pausing frequently so that Maya could translate it for Derek.

Kavalappara was a calf when he was brought by the aristocratic Nair family of Kavalappara. It was rumoured that his mother was killed when trying to cross over a railway line. This story had its origins in Kavalappara, with his uncontrollable temper, chasing and attempting to knock down the carriages of a moving train. He was a magnificent animal much admired for his size, towering a foot above the others. Named Chakravarty meaning king, he was lovingly referred to as Kuttan. Not that he had an affectionate spirit. On the other hand, he was extremely aggressive and untameable. No chains could hold him, and all those who attempted to tame his waywardness came to a grim end. The first to be gored to death was Kelu Nambiar, a strong and well-experienced mahout, who attempted to tame his high spirits by beating him with a stick. The family panicked. They knew they had adopted a wild, unrestrainable beast. So, they gifted him to the Kudal Manikyam temple in Irinjalakuda. They hoped that God would mend his ways. By now, the elephant with his huge, scythe-shaped, glistening tusks had earned the name of Komban Kavalappara. The spate of killings continued. Some say he killed sixteen men; others swore it was twenty-two. Each time he gored and savagely killed these men, he would go and bathe in the temple pond. This ritualistic act of purification by a killer elephant was much talked about, as he exhibited no other form of remorse.

One day, Kunnjan Nair, a mahout by profession, happened to see Kavalappara. Impressed by his air of majesty, he bought him. He was undeterred by his reputation as a killer and showered him with love. For many years, the tenuous bond between the man and the beast remained unbroken by the bouts of rage in which, Kavalappara had taken so many lives. However, even during this period, it was apparent that in a procession, when the elephants were lined up, Kavalappara had to take the lead position or there would inevitably be a display of rage. Kunnjan Nair had a chain made, which was three times the thickness of the chain used to shackle elephants, and thus prevented any untoward incident from occurring.

Destiny arrives in many shapes, as it did for Komban Kavalappara. Kunnjan Nair was invited to participate in the festival with Komban in Thiruvanchikulam, a Shiva temple in Kodungallur. It was assumed by all concerned that the idol of the lord would be mounted on Kavalappara, who was resplendent in his prime. However, the Maharaja of Kochi refused to give the pride of place to Kavalappara. He ordered that his elephant be allowed to lead in the temple festival. The moment Kavalappara sighted the other elephant, in front of him, his fury broke loose. He attacked the lead elephant and then broke free of his chains. He did not attack anyone else, but Kunnjan Nair was not taking any chances. He moved forward to quieten Kavalappara, who gently pushed him aside with his trunk. Then, Nair hit him across his trunk with a stick and the infuriated elephant gored him to death. Realising moments later that he had brutally killed the only man he loved, Kavalappara stood embracing Kunnjan Nair with his trunk. He rampaged through the town of Kodungallur, which resembled a ghost town, all having fled indoors. Finally, on the orders of the Maharaja of Kochi, Kavalappara was shot by British soldiers.

Derek listened avidly, nodding his head to indicate his interest. Kartyayani Amma ended the song and lay down deeply exhausted. Leela would have lifted her, but Derek bent down and gathered the old woman. Cradling her in his arms, he followed Leela, gently laying her on her mattress.

Nina and Maya exchanged glances. Maya rose as if to leave, and Derek followed. Holding him back, Nina turned to Leela, a question in her eyes. Leela looked away and unlatched the door. She sighed.

"It is a long story, Nina. I will come with amma, tomorrow."

On the drive back home, they sat in silence. Roy made a few conversational sallies which Derek answered politely. There had been an awkward moment earlier when Roy had opened the front door of the car and playfully scooped Nina to put her down on the front seat.

Nina had jumped out and linking arms with Derek announced, "My husband. Derek meet Roy, Maya chechi's son, and my cousin."

The men had shaken hands, Roy looking nonplussed while Derek wore a shuttered expression.

In the back seat, Nina welded herself against Derek. Derek held her hand loosely on his lap. His jeans were damp with rain, but Nina could feel the heat of his manhood as he began to massage the mound of Venus under her thumb. When Nina looked up, she saw that Roy was watching them intently in the rearview mirror. Derek must have noticed it too. He let go of Nina's hand and began to talk to Maya chechi about the rainwater drains which could be found in several parts of Kerala. On his way, he had seen school boys fishing in these drains with a length of twine and a bait of some sort, normally an earthworm, attached to a pin.

"Most children are cruel because empathy is a quality they learn over time," said Maya chechi.

"That and the fact that children live at the biological level like all animals. They enjoy themselves without restraint, and at the same time harbour no prejudices. They can be both cruel and generous till civilization gets to them."

"Nina and you would make excellent parents," remarked Maya chechi looking back over her shoulders at them.

"I am ready whenever Nina is," said Derek.

Nina was startled. What was with Derek? They had never discussed parenthood as a possibility at any time in the future. And what was with Roy pulling a face as if he had just bitten on something sour? The air in the car was crackling and it was not from the storm alone.

Nina frowned at Roy who was looking at her quizzically. He winked at her in the mirror and grinned.

Roy had always been the brother she never had. There had been a short period when Roy, a gawky fourteen-year-old, had been infatuated with her. He had declared his love for her as they sat on steps made of logs of coconut which descended into a pond. Nina had been drawing faces in the sand, and when she sat up in surprise, he tried to plant a kiss on her cheek. His face was flushed with embarrassment, and the acne which studded his face made his skin look striated. Nina had gently pushed him away and asked whether she could treat his skin. Four years older than Roy she had sensed his changed regard but had thought it a mere adolescent crush, best ignored. As she felt him shudder in mortification, she gently held his hand. They sat for a while longer, their hands linked. The silence stretched taut between them until Roy suddenly wrenched his hand away and bolted. His breath had been ragged, and Nina had thought she heard him bite back a sob before he fled. She sat a little longer wondering how she could make it right. The only way was to behave as if nothing had happened. He could then retrieve the remnants of his dignity. But, Nina was not to meet him for a long time.

Nina had left to do an aesthetician's course at Chelsford Institute in London. A few years later, she heard that he had left for a graduate program in graphic design at Rhodes University. They were friends on Facebook, and he always seemed to be partying. In most of the pictures, there was an attractive, Bohemian-looking girl with him. When he did return after graduation, he never went back. He took over the very profitable business of manufacturing and supplying dental implants.

The car bumped to a halt bringing Nina's reverie to an end. She got out quickly, but not before Roy had opened the door and reached out to retrieve her bag for her. He placed it on her shoulder, his thumb moving across the skin on her forearm. Startled, she looked up, but his expression was bland. She backed away giving him one swift kick on his shin before walking into the house. Derek followed a step behind. He stopped to admire the wooden ceiling and the still glossy, slate, blue floors.

He looked at Maya and asked, "Are you planning major changes to the house?"

Maya said, "What you see is a beautiful shell. The hollow remains of what was once a beautiful tharavadu veedu. It is being eaten by termites. The materials and craftsmen for restoring this old, decrepit house are scarce. So…" her voice trailed off.

"I have a friend at the Laurie Baker Centre," asserted Derek. " They have expanded into low-cost renovations for old homes. I will speak to him, and he will come and take a look."

Roy butted in, "It will cost a ton to restore, and for half that cost we can build a new house with all the modern amenities. This gloomy place with its shadows and the hall of the dead is better razed to the ground."

The way Roy bent his head and pawed the ground as he spoke reminded Derek of the threat display of a bull. Derek decided he would not engage with Roy, in an act of male dominance, by being overtly assertive in taking control of the situation.

He picked up his suitcase and turned to Nina, who took him towards her room. She heard Maya chechi say something to Roy in a raised voice. Then she closed their door, dropped her bag and hugged Derek, who had his back turned. He quickly spun around around and kissed the top of her head. They stood like that for a while, Nina basking in the warmth of his hold and that masculine smell, a mixture of sweat and something else. Pheromones, Derek had once said, were typically emitted by the males of many species during mating time. Nina had extremely sharp olfactory senses, and she was ovulating. She could feel Derek's erection as she slowly rubbed herself against him. He cupped her face and kissed the hollow of her neck, before reaching her mouth. He was like a man who had gone thirsty for far too long. The sharp knock at the door startled them, and they sprang apart. Roy stood at the door glowering.

"Dinner in fifteen," he announced before closing the door with a snap.

Nina was furious. Why was the normally affable Roy acting like a bear which was stung by bees?

Derek raised his eyebrows, grinned and asked, "Is Roy always so territorial? Or is it just something about me?"

Derek was not bothered, Nina realised. He was a man who accepted that people would not necessarily follow a pattern. Living among tribals, he knew that socially ritualistic behaviour lubricated the wheels of all societies. Even monkeys smiled in appeasement. Their smile was to express peaceful intent when a subordinate approached a more dominant member of the group. Humans signalled subordination by bowing, grovelling, saluting, laughing at the other's jokes and not expressing their opinion unless it was explicitly sought. Conviviality likewise expressed itself in eye contact which held only for four or five seconds, hugging, eating, drinking and laughing together. Roy had by his barely veiled hostility signalled that Derek was unwelcome. His blatant flirtation with Nina, the holding of a glance longer than necessary was combative.

Nina was confused. Roy had a series of flings which had petered out. That, she knew from the occasional gossip about the family when she was visiting her mother. Roy had never made any attempt to contact her when he returned to India to take over his father's business. She had met him only once since then. This was at a cousin's wedding in Bangalore. Derek had not accompanied her, though, by then, they were already living together. Nina loved to dance, and Roy had been her partner in all the dances. Their dance moves were so sensual and well-coordinated, that the onlookers began clapping and whistling their appreciation. Not then, nor when he had come to pick her up from the airport, had there been a suggestion on Roy's part that he was attracted to her.

Nina led Derek to the dark, cavernous dining hall lit by a single tube light. Maya apologised for the frugality of the fare. Nina laughed, and Derek joined her in teasing Maya. The table was groaning under the weight of the array of dishes, which the live-in maid had laid on it, in carefully polished silverware.

Maya turned to Derek and asked him about his conservation work while ladling some fish curry into his plate. Derek appreciated its subtle aromas and the flavour imparted by kodampuli, the Malabar tamarind. Of Roy, there was no sign. Nina had heard raised voices while she was hastily untangling and braiding her wind-swept hair. Maya chechi, she knew would not countenance disrespect to a guest. A woman of refinement, Maya chechi believed firmly in the adage that a guest was an emissary of God. Moreover, Nina and she had an undeniable bond, which now included Derek. Nina was more than a little surprised when Roy joined them. He did not glance her way, but seating himself on Derek's right, he asked him whether he was involved in the programmes for turtle conservation in India.

Derek responded that he was overseeing the research programme at the Indian Institute of Science related to the skewed sex ratio among the hatchlings of the olive ridley turtle.

Maya wanted to know more about the conservation program.

Roy said, "It is that program in Orissa that I had signed up for just before leaving for Rhodes."

Derek added, "The olive ridley turtles are a threatened species. For years, they have been laying their eggs along the Orissa coastline. After laying the eggs, the turtles return to the sea. One of the strangest phenomena in nature is that of baby turtles making straight for the sea as soon as they hatch. Some manage to traverse the distance, but most fall prey to predators… jackals, hyenas, stray dogs, birds and humans. The market for the meat, shell, leather and eggs of turtles is very lucrative." He stopped with a sigh.

Derek was not loquacious, and now fatigue descended upon him like a blanket. He had travelled for several hours, catching a red-eye flight because, for once, he was the anxious one. Nina had sounded very unlike herself. When he was on one of his several trips away from home, she would pursue him with calls. On his tiger trails, he left recorded messages, just in case he could not answer her calls. Anxiety was an inherited trait, and it could not be willed away. In those who suffered from its sharp claws, anxiety was an expression of love. Nina, an only child, had to constantly persuade her mother that she was adult enough to ensure her own safety. It probably had not occurred to Nina that she was exhibiting learned behaviour when she sent out her anxiety signals. Made vulnerable by love and afraid of loss, people with anxiety syndrome imagined the worst scenario for their loved ones. Derek had come to realise that the need to stay connected was not a form of monitoring. For Nina and her mother, it was a coping mechanism. Contrary, though it was by fearing loss, they attempted to prevent such an occurrence. Derek had moved over the years from impatience to acceptance. He was surprised that Nina had not badgered him to accompany her, on her visit to Kerala, to meet Maya. Something, he had not had time for since their marriage. Maya, or Maya chechi as Nina called her was saying something.

"What about the efforts to make hunting and selling of turtles unlawful."

"Yes, there is. A lot of funding too. But it has been a real challenge roping in the fishing communities. During mating seasons, many adults are accidentally caught in trawl nests, and that single process has reduced their numbers drastically. They are on the brink of extinction." Derek paused, too tired to go on.

Maya failed to get the cue. She met so few people who shared her interest that she continued the conversation with, "And funding?"

"Their survival has been made possible by WWF India, some non-governmental organisations and as I mentioned, international funding. With advocacy and the promise of money, the village fishing communities have been roped in to play guardians."

Nina said, "Let's go there, Derek. It would be fun to see those hatchlings especially when they begin to move their flippers on reaching water."

Derek smiled. "No promises, Nina. They have clamped down on visitors. Just too many tourists were milling around, taking selfies to post. Ugh! What a prig I sound. I have nothing against selfies… it's just that tourists deter conservation efforts. They came in droves to watch the spectacular sight of hundreds of baby turtles making their way back to the sea. The government had to put a stop to it when they discovered that smuggling of turtles was taking place in the guise of tourism."

Turning to Roy, Derek asked, "Have you been there?"

"More than a decade ago. I stayed in a small town in Orissa called Ganjam. I was a part of a project which was monitoring their nesting near Rushikulya river. This was when the Wildlife Institute of India called for volunteers to tag turtles and collect data."

Helping himself to the delectable handmade chocolates his mother got from a friend in Kottayam, he added, "Amma, do you remember the short film I made to educate the local community on how best to protect sea turtles? You were fascinated. It was for the most part fun, and the fishermen often took us for their pre-dawn fishing expeditions, where I got exclusive photo shoots that later featured in National Geography."

Since both the men were keen lensmen, the rest of the meal was consumed with the talk of the best ways to weave narratives using photographic images with Roy doing the most talking.

Nina's head had begun to droop with exhaustion.

Maya gestured towards her and sang under her breath, "To bed, to bed says sleepy head."

Derek sprang up, and Nina followed him out of the room stumbling over the wooden ledges which separated the rooms in the house. Roy, who was just behind, caught her by the arm. Their eyes met and held. Roy's expression was unfathomable. Nina could not recognise in him the affable, laid-back cousin who had picked her up from the airport. She followed Derek and fell into bed before he could turn off the lights. Sometime later she awoke, feeling constricted by the clothes she had fallen asleep in. Easing herself out of the bed, she peeled them off. She did not want to switch on the lights to ferret out nightwear. In any case, she slept more soundly nude. She snuggled up against Derek, turning to lie with her back against him. The room was cold, with the air conditioner in the coolest mode. She shivered as she drew the blanket over her head, gasping as Derek moved against her. He entered her from behind, prising her legs apart. She placed her knee in a position which allowed him to penetrate more deeply and began to moan. Dennis was a considerate lover who never skipped the foreplay. He moved roughly now, his hands clasped over her breasts. They were both too hungry for entrees thought Nina. He did not wait this time for her to cry out as she orgasmed. He was not holding back, and Nina bit her lips to hold back her scream as he slumped against her, his heart beating rapidly against her shoulder blades. She felt waves rising from the tips of her toes in electric spirals to her core. Then all was still.

Nina lay wide awake. It always took her a while to sleep after they made love. Derek on the other hand, slept more soundly. Now, he lay on his back, and to

Nina's dismay began to snore. She pushed him onto his side and tried to find a more comfortable position. The room had grown warm. Throwing off the blanket, she went to shut the window which seemed to have swung open on its own. It was the one she had not been able to latch. The windows were secured by hooks, and the hook on that window was warped with age.

Where was the caduceus? She could not feel its familiar weight against her hips. She wore it, strung on a thick string like the kind with which they tied amulets to babies. She slid off the bed and searched frantically among the heap of clothes on the floor. Nothing. Going down on all fours, she crept around the bed. It lay half across the room, glimmering wickedly in the shaft of light which entered through the partially open window. Pulling it hastily over her head, she shook Derek awake. He sat bolt upright, and in a minute ceased the situation. His senses had learnt to filter out normal sounds. In escaping the perils of tracking wild animals, Derek was alert to changes in his environment. The partially open window and Nina's agitation communicated a panicked urgency. On the verandah into which the window opened, Derek found muddy footprints. They were still wet. Someone had stood there, just moments ago, coming in out of the rain. There were footprints leading to the door but not away from it. There was however within easy stride, a cloth streaked with mud. Whoever stood at the window had wiped both feet to evade detection. Which way could the intruder have gone?

Outside, the pelting rain had wiped out all clues. Derek put his fingers to his lips and pointed to the stairway. Someone was descending on hushed feet. Putting his arms around Nina, who had begun to shiver, Derek turned to find Roy standing at the foot of the stairs, a golf club in hand. He halted when he saw them and plonked himself down on the last stair. Derek told him of what had just transpired.

Roy shook his head. "Lots of factories have closed, and petty thefts are on the rise in the neighbourhood. They steal anything they can lay their hands on. The modus operandi is to insert a long stick through an open window and draw out objects within its reach. Nina's arrival has been noticed. The thief must have come in the hope of finding something of value lying around. Don't tell amma about it. She is on the verge of asking for police protection," he chuckled.

"Can I make a nightcap for you? Some stiff brandy would do Nina good."

They followed him to his room which was an even bigger mess than when Nina had last entered it.

As he was pouring out the brandy, Nina remarked about the beautiful crystal ware which contained the liquor.

"Dad's collection," said Roy.

Derek glanced over the room. Though things were not stacked carefully, there was a certain order despite the seeming untidiness. The books, arranged in heaps, were segregated subject-wise. Everything was within the occupant's easy reach with total disregard for aesthetics.

Roy held out a brandy snifter with about one and a half ounces of brandy "Best drunk neat," he commented.

Derek warmed the brandy between his palms and took a small sip. Nina downed hers like a shot and spluttered as it singed the back of her throat.

"A second?" asked Roy moving to fill her glass. It was his stride which caught Derek's attention. It was smooth and muscular like a panther's. Then, he noticed that the pyjamas under the long dressing gown, Roy wore, were rolled up. But, not far enough. The folds at the back of his shins were encrusted with mud.

Nina waved Roy away. She looked flustered. Derek gulped his drink quickly, and they got up to leave.

"Good night. Let's keep it from amma," he reiterated.

Dawn was just breaking, and the canopy of palms glinted a dull gold. Nina hastened Derek out of the house, and for a while, they stood drinking in the distinct smells of early morning. A solitary bird could be heard chirping from a nearby bush, followed by another further up in the grove. Soon the bird chorus would begin. Derek could feel Nina's nails bite into his forearm as they walked through rain-cleansed, moist air. He seated himself on a cement bench at the very edge of the clearing. The rest of the ground was tangled undergrowth.

"Reptile land," stated Derek. "Trespassing strictly prohibited."

He had seen a shimmering, long form sliding away. Just under the bench was something which appeared like transparent nylon netting; a snake's shed skin. Not the right moment Derek decided for a lesson in zoology. Snakes in any case did not linger long around humans. Naturally shy, rarely did they attack, unless provoked.

Nina began to speak. She began with their meeting with the Israeli couple leading to an entire series of startling and unfathomable events.

Nina paused to catch her breath, looking over her shoulder at the thicket which guarded them like a wall. It was almost impenetrable and too low for anyone to lie hidden.

"It all began with the caduceus. Once sighted and recognised, it has set off something… a pursuit. I am being pursued, and I don't know what to do next," she lamented.

"Put it back in the locker?"

"No," said Nina. "It will not end there. The word has got around. Someone wants it badly. But someone else does not want it taken away from us, our family. Some protective forces that I cannot discern. Or are there rivals contending for the caduceus?"

"Is it worth risking your life, your… our dreams?"

"Derek, if it is an amulet, let us save it for…," her voice tapered off.

"Our children? The next of kin?".

The silence grew until it threatened to engulf them. Derek had made it very evident, at the start of their relationship, that he did not want a child. Nina had always wanted children, and at the beginning had thought she could talk him into it when she could afford a child. Her work consumed her, and there had never been a right time. But there were times when she grew broody. Her insistence that they consider parenthood would send Derek scuttling. Or he would retreat behind a wall she could not climb. Derek had a younger sibling with Down's syndrome and an older brother who had committed suicide, after being sodomised, at the rather prestigious school to which he had been sent. The matter had been hushed.

His parents were the first of the Anglo-Indian community to migrate to Australia with their youngest child. Australia offered better opportunities for children with special needs. Derek stayed back. It was a relief for him to strike a path away from the gloom that his parents had lived through. He willed himself to stop feeling guilty and launched into a career of safeguarding other species from being annihilated by the greed of men. He believed that the human populace had far outgrown the numbers which could be sustained by the resources available on earth. By stealth and cunning, however, humans kept taking what was not theirs leading to the growing conflict with animals.

Nina was looking away, her expression tight and constrained. He tried to take her hand, but she pulled away and stood up, her mind in turmoil. She had been off the pill all of the month. She had not expected Derek to join her. She could take the 'morning after' pill but knew she would not want to. They would just have to see, would they not? This, Nina thought, could be the fork in their relationship. She knew she was not acting rationally, but something hard and defiant arose within her. She choked and began to cough. Evading Derek's hand as he reached out to pat her back, she ran up the steps to join Maya chechi. She was threading tulsi leaves into a garland to send to the Kodungallur Bhagavathi temple.

Maya looked up from her task and wondered why Nina was looking so spent. An all-nighter making up for the separation? Bhagavathi, Bhagavathi, where were her thoughts wandering even as she set about stringing the tulsi malai?

They perched on the veranda alongside her. After observing her silently for a few minutes, Derek began twisting the tulsi leaves deftly into a garland. Nina sat gazing at the pond, swinging her feet back and forth.

"Who are these for?" asked Derek.

"Kodungallur Bhagavathi."

"Do you go to the temple daily?"

"Somedays, I just send these. But I string them daily."

"Lots of legends about the place."

"Which one have you heard?"

"I read a brief write-up about Kovalan and Kannagi. Is Kannagi, Bhagavathi?"

Maya unconsciously switched on her lecture mode as she embarked on the story. She was starved for listeners and in Derek she had always found a good listener.

"The story occurs in a classic epic Silappathikaran where Kovalan is accused wrongly of stealing the queen's anklet and attempting to sell it. He was the son of a rich merchant who had spent all his money on a courtesan. He returned to a forgiving wife, and the couple made their way to Madurai in the hope of recovering their lost fortune. They were in dire need of some capital to make a fresh beginning. Kannagi offered her jewel-studded anklets, and Kovalan took one of them to the market. The merchant, who he tried to sell it to, believed them to be the queen's anklet. He was dragged to the palace, and the king without enquiring any further had him beheaded."

"Our courts would have suited Kannan better. He would have become a grey beard before all was done," quipped Derek.

"Whoever says justice delayed is justice denied hasn't heard this story," added Nina, looking up with a smile at Derek.

Nina had time to recover, and her heart reached out to Derek. He was so genuinely interested in people. She could see that Maya chechi had gravitated towards him, sunning herself in his warmth. Derek gave totally of himself, and that was the reason she felt neglected at times.

Taking the finished garland from his hand, Maya said, "Kannagi was distraught and demanded an audience with the king. She removed the other anklet and broke it open to show that it was filled with emeralds, rubies and other precious stones. The queen's anklets had mere pearls in them. Her wrath set the city ablaze and everything turned to ashes. As she walked away, Kannagi threw her anklet into the air. It landed at the spot where the Bhagavathi temple was situated. Kannagi came and worshipped at the shrine of Bhadrakali, another name for Bhagavathi, and merged with her."

Pausing to collect her thoughts, Maya continued, "To many, she is a presence in their lives as palpable as the family one lives with. Many start their day visiting her shrine to seek her blessing. Some go to vent… to confide their tales of woe and come away comforted."

Nina chipped in, "There are legends galore about Kodungallur amma, but the one I like best is about the traveller. I heard this one from my mother. Do you know, Derek, that for a long time, Nambudiris did not build their houses in Kodungallur? Their homes were always situated on the other side of the bridge which spans the river."

"The one you cross before entering Kodungallur? Why is that," asked Derek.

"A traveller once came to Kodungallur. He wanted food and shelter for the night, He knocked on the doors of the Nambudiris, priests of the Bhagavathi temple. Their homes lay at the entry point, just after the bridge is crossed, close to the temple. But they turned him away. Hungry and tired, he walked on and came to a dwelling. A woman opened the door. She asked him to bathe, before eating, in a pond nearby. The story goes that she took her shoolam and drew a circle on the ground."

Derek enquired, "Shoolam?"

"That is what they call the spear she holds in one of her hands. This became a pond, where the weary traveller could bathe and refresh himself. The traveller was served a veritable feast. After having his fill, he thanked the gracious lady of the house and went to sleep. When he awoke, he found himself sleeping in the Bhagavathi Temple. Realising that his hostess had been none other than Kodungallur amma, he prostrated before the deity in deep gratitude. Just then, the head priest entered. He had been punished for his lack of hospitality. His home and the adjoining homes of all Nambudiris had been burnt to cinders. The priest entered and bowed before the traveller, seeking his forgiveness."

The dog barked from its kennel in front of the house. Maya raised her head. An early visitor? They could hear someone's tread. Both Nina and Derek rose and returned to their room. Nina lay down and promptly plunged into sleep. Derek sat in the space beside her and opened his laptop. There were a few urgent emails to be sent. He had left in a hurry. Someone needed to take over the reins of administration until he returned, He did not know when he would get back. There were more important claims on his time; the chase was gaining momentum, and Nina would fight to the finish. The caduceus was at the center of it all. But, was there more?

There was a gentle knock at the door. Derek heard it, but he was in the midst of rummaging through his suitcase, in the adjoining room, for something washed to wear. Wild-lifers travelled light, and he had set out with an urgency which had left no time for packing. Derek got up and moved softly to see who had come. He was not noticed by the man who had entered the room. Roy stood gazing at Nina, who lay curled up tight like a foetus. He bent forward as if to stroke her cheek. Straightening up, he found Derek watching him from the other side of the room. With no show of embarrassment, he addressed Derek.

"Leela chechi has come to meet Nina. Amma sent me to call you both for breakfast."

Nina sat up. She felt like she had a hangover. And what was Roy doing in her room? Why was Derek looking like he had seen an unidentified beetle? Roy held out his hand as if to help her up. His eyes had a look of concern. Nina evaded his hand, sitting bolt upright in bed. Roy repeated the message, his face returning to that of a polite stranger. The atmosphere in the room was thick enough to saw. Nina lay back and was slowly drifting back to sleep when a knock came again. This time Maya chechi entered with Leela in tow.

"She has something to say to you," Maya said, glancing across at Derek. Derek made as if to leave. Maya stopped him.

"Listen to Leela, Derek. If you abandon the quest after you hear her story, take Nina with you. Or stay by her side till she calls it quits."

Chapter XI
A Tale of Two Births

Leela looked at Nina and asked in Malayalam, "How many months is it?"

"Is what?" asked Nina.

"Pregnant?" Leela queried in English.

Derek's head shot up and he looked quizzically from one to the other.

"No," Nina replied looking startled.

"You have that lustre which comes to women in the early days of their pregnancy," said Leela.

Seeing Nina's discomfiture, Maya intervened, "You think of nothing else," she chided. "Now, what is it you wanted to say?"

"This is about two births and a death."

"What does that have to do with Nina?" said Maya.

Leela did not flinch. She was staring straight at Nina.

"Nani Kutty, your great-grandmother had a twin brother."

"Was that other child stillborn?" asked Nina.

"He was a beautiful baby, like the baby girl and very much alive. The Jewess had a stillborn baby."

"Which Jewess?" asked Maya. "Leela, what is with you? Don't subject us to these riddles. Breakfast is waiting so be quick about it."

Maya glanced apologetically at Derek. She was appalled at Leela asking intrusive questions and then speaking utter gibberish. Perhaps, she ought to have sent her away.

The room was quiet for a few moments. Nina was thrown by Leela's assumption. Could it be true? Her periods had always been irregular unless she was on the pill. She had lost count of the number of weeks which had passed. She had been looking for answers to explain the chase, which began with the attention the caduceus had drawn. The excitement of the chase, of being a quarry, had expelled everything except keeping ahead of the game. But had she? Leela had begun to speak, halting at first, and then the words poured out of her like blood from a wound that could not be staunched.

"Ammini Amma, or Radha as she was called by her family, was your great-great-grandmother. She went into labour and was being attended to by Kartyayani Amma's mother who was barely seven years old. She had a close bond with Radha and had come along with her mother. The girl was asked to wet Radha's mouth with water every time a contraction subsided, and Radha entered the twilight zone, where for a few minutes a woman experiences freedom from pain. Looking up from wiping Radha's clammy forehead, the girl noticed a white face pressed against the window. She shrieked out aloud, and her mother, the midwife came in from the next room where she had been resting for a few moments. Radha's labour had been a long and protracted one, but the midwife noticed that she was still hours away from giving birth. Someone was tapping at the window. She threw the window open and was startled to see a woman, who was obviously in labour, her white mundu covered with the discharge from her bleeding womb. The woman held out her hand in supplication. The midwife alerted the household, and the thampuran ordered that she be taken in, and a place found for her to deliver her child safely."

"You speak as if it happened just yesterday," said Derek.

"Yesterday, or a century ago, midwives know about strange events which occurred during the birthing of the babies of the tharavadu. It is handed down from mother to daughter. Secrecy is essential. I would not have spoken but for Maya chechi. She takes care of us as my mother would have if she had been alive." Leela began to weep, swaying back and forth.

"Stop this nonsense, Leela. What happened so long ago will not hurt you. It might help us on the other hand. Go on. And no interruptions," said Maya looking at Derek.

"Since the thampuran's estate was near the port, Damon had managed to send word to Radha through the ships which arrived there. After the Periyar River flooded, the port in Cranganore became less accessible. The majority of trade was diverted to Cochin. Some continued to dock further down the coast and patronise the town of Cranganore, where they felt the spices were more varied and aromatic. Damon had been one of those." Leela was prevaricating.

Maya interrupted, "Who was this woman?"

"A Jewess. She was on her way to Mattancherry, the Jewish town in Cochin, to deliver the baby. Some Arab traders, who had a long-drawn trade rivalry with the Jews, attacked her husband. She fled before they turned on her. Noticing a light at the thampuran's house, she went there hoping to find shelter and help."

She paused and asked for water. After a few sips, she laid her glass aside and said with a sigh, "My great-grandmother kept silent, never disclosing what she had witnessed. But there were others present at that birth. Radha had twins. A boy and a girl. The Jewess delivered a male child, a stillborn."

Leela seemed unable to go on. She pleaded with them never to reveal what would bring shame to her family. Midwifery was a family trade. A scandal would ruin them. After a few moments of silence, she began to speak again. Her words came out in a rush. She paused, caught her breath and began again.

"The midwife snipped the umbilical cord of the twins, and wrapped them snugly, before placing them in Radha's arms. Radha took out the gold chain she wore around her neck. The pendant on it was different from the conventional tali worn by other Nair women. It had the design of intertwined snakes embedded with jewels. She had got it specially crafted by a goldsmith. It was a replica of the one, she wore on a thread, around her hips. She put the gold chain she wore around her neck on the baby boy and asked the midwife to put the other pendant, strung on thread, on the little girl. Radha then fell into a deep slumber."

Leela rose as if to go. Maya chechi pushed her gently back into the chair and said, "Go on."

Leela continued the recitation. It was as if she was recounting a story, each word of which had been memorised.

"The midwife laid the babies down in the cradle and turned around to attend to the other woman, writhing in pain. The thampuran's sister had brought her in, and she lay on a mat, placed at the entry to the room. The room was dark, and the midwife was old and exhausted. The Jewess was a Pardeshi Jew, and the loss of blood had made her as white as the sheet on which she lay. She had no strength to bear down. The midwife felt her way in and pulled the baby out with one swoop. He did not cry; it was his mother whose screams reverberated through the house. The thampuran's sister snatched the inert baby from the midwife's arms and threw it into the heap of soiled rags in the corner. Before anyone else could move, she picked up Radha's sleeping infant, the boy, and placed it in the arms of the Jewess. The midwife fought to take the baby from her, but the thampuran's sister knocked her down with a blow."

Leela paused and looked at them with rage burning in her eyes. My mother was not a witness. She has merely heard about the switching of the babies. She now lives in a twilight zone, where the past rises to confront her and she believes she has sinned."

"But why did Janaki do that?" Nina asked in bewilderment.

"Because she wanted her retarded son to become the thampuran," said Leela.

"What claim would Radha's babies have to the thampuran's property?" asked Derek.

"Marumakkathayam."

"What is that?" asked Derek.

"It is the social system which was prevalent in the Nair community of Kerala. A matrilineal system. Property was entirely owned by the women in the family, and the name of the family, its special identity in the clan, was perpetuated through these women. The eldest male member was however regarded as the head of the family. So, in that respect, it continued to be patriarchal," explained Maya.

Leela said, "The thampuran's sister had always nursed a grievance against Radha. She was the youngest of her cousins and much admired for her beauty. It was Radha's sister whom the thampuran had married. She was his mora ponnu."

Derek looked mystified but did not want to interrupt Leela again.

It was Roy who caught that look and said, "Marriage between cousins was allowed in Kerala. The children of two sisters are regarded as siblings. The children of a brother and sister are not. They can marry. In fact, when a girl was of an age to marry, it was the uncle's son, who in the past, had the first claim to her hand. She was his mora ponnu. This social norm was primarily to keep the property within the family."

Nina was startled. When had Roy entered the room, and how much had he heard? Why was she uncomfortable with his presence? When had his warm affability changed into a baffling, dark inscrutability? She glanced at Derek who looked unsurprised by his presence.

Leela continued, "When the first thampuratti died, Radha was to marry the thampuran. But she married a videshi sailor, whose children were the twins my great- great grandmother helped to bring into the world. Radha was as much entitled to the property as the thampuran's sister was. Her daughter too would be entitled to it one day, but neither of their sons could claim a share of the sprawling acres of fecund land. The very heart of the spice country. However, one of them could become the patriarch. The thampuran's sister had a child with a large, misshapen head. He would never be normal. By giving the male child away, she had cleared the deck for her son."

The room was silent for a long while. The grandfather clock in the hall could be heard chiming the hour. Then, all of them began to speak at once.

Nina said, "Was the little baby girl, Nani Kutty? Is the caduceus I have, the one Radha wore around her hips? Like I do now? Was she scared it would be stolen? Why did she make an identical one? Was it because she knew she would bear twins? And how did they explain the loss of the other child?"

Derek was perturbed. There was definitely an air of heightened excitement in the room. He could smell a predator in the room, but who?

Derek cut in with, "Go on, Leela."

"Radha had little time to grieve for the child she had lost. She had hardly recovered from the birthing of her twins when there came news that the vessel, in which Damos was sailing back to Muziris, had been lost in a storm. There were no survivors. Radha sank into depression, her milk dried up, and a wet nurse had to be brought in for the child."

Leela rose to go. Maya pressed her to stay, but she hurried away.

PART – 3

At the source of the longest river

The voice of the hidden waterfall

And the children in the apple-tree

Not known, because not looked for

But heard, half-heard, in the stillness

Between two waves of the sea.

—T S Eliot, from "Little Giddings",
Four Quartets.

Chapter XII

Venice of the East

Nina stirred her foot to distract the small, silvery fish which were nibbling her feet. Derek was happily floating on his back, watching the cumulus clouds drift. The pond had been cleaned after the men came to fish stealthily at night. Now, the water was a clear, limpid green. There was a flash of tiny, blue wings which Nina mistook for a butterfly till it perched on the coconut tree, which grew across the pond as if bowing in perpetual obeisance to the waters below. Derek had grown still as he watched the kingfisher. Within the blink of an eye, it swooped down into the pond and flew back into one of the holes, which punctured the sides of the pond, a sliver of silverfish in its mouth. Was this what Radha had seen as she sat by the pond with the man she had fallen in love with? He had been in her life only for a season, while generations of the kingfisher had remained eternally wedded to the terrain. Nina shook her head. She knew from Derek that nature was self-absorbed and much of animal behaviour was wired for survival. Watching him as he floated closer to her, she wondered how he could be so passionate and yet, unsentimental. He hoisted her on his back before she could protest and swam across the pond. Nina let the tension evaporate from her as she allowed herself to be carried to where the fledglings were. She could feel his muscles working under her as he swam past the nest burrowed in the sand.

Nina said, "Let us go to Mattancherry."

"Journey's end?" asked Derek.

Nina nodded against his back, digging in her chin until Derek squealed.

"And the caduceus?" he asked plonking her back on the step.

"Goes back to the locker," she shrugged.

"For the progeny?" Derek was squinting his eyes against the sunlight which had grown more intense.

Nina looked away, digging her toes into the sand.

"Yes," said Derek. He repeated, "For our progeny."

Nina looked up, startled. She read the affirmation in his eyes. He knew. His trained eye had read the subtle changes in her body, the brain fog and evasiveness. He just knew, in the same way, Leela had. Nina leaned forward to rest her forehead against him. This was a reprieve. No painful decisions to be made. She felt dizzy with relief.

"Not sure yet, Derek."

"Barkis is willin', Nina."

Nina doubled over with laughter and felt the tension seep through her feet into the water, swirling around her ankles.

Maya brought several, oil-stained packets for them to pack. A variety of chips and the local, black wheat halwa. Nina and Derek protested in vain. Maya would have none of it. Since they were catching a flight to Bangalore, they could ensure the goodies reached Nina's mother at Mysore.

Nina knew there was nothing more to be learned by lingering at Kodungallur. They would go to the Jew town in Mattancherry, more out of curiosity to see the locale, which had figured in the tale that had unravelled, than with the hope of further leads. Derek wanted to spend a day drifting through the famed backwaters of Alleppey. Called the 'Venice of the East', its varied ecosystem was irresistible for a naturalist. Maya had made all the arrangements for them. Nina tried persuading her to accompany them. Maya would have none of it. She never left the tharavadu. Who would light the lamp at the shrine of Nagarajava if she left even for a day? Roy had gone on a business trip without bidding them goodbye. Nina felt snubbed. Where had all their previous camaraderie gone, she wondered. Derek seemed completely indifferent to his absence, so Nina did not bring it up with him.

The backwaters were grey where they swept against the granite of the pier. Nina scruffed her toes against the edge while peering into the murky depths below. All around them were houseboats, tethered to the shore with thick ropes tied to iron poles, dotting the pier at equal intervals. Painted in gaudy colours, they had very creative names. Fascinated, Nina read out their names; Queen Angel, Genesis, Treemonks… as she slowly walked down. Stopping momentarily to watch a skiff pass, she jumped as someone touched her shoulder, all senses alert. It was Roy.

"What on earth are you doing here?" she shot out.

"Relax," grinned Roy. "Amma sent me to play escort. My friend owns a good boat. There it is, at the end of the pier. Your husband, however, is feeding the gulls and would not notice if a meteor strikes you."

Nina winced. Roy had sensed what Nina strove to accept. Derek's total involvement with whatever had his passionate regard, to the exclusion of all else. She had often asked herself, whether the measure of a relationship was not in terms of how it weighed against competing interests.

Meeting Roy's gaze, she retorted, "What is it to you anyway? You are deluding yourself if you think there was anything between us. It is only, now, very suddenly, that you seem to have unearthed some fragments of adolescent passion. Why are you bent on destroying any vestige of the friendly regard, we once had?"

"My emotions have taken me by surprise, Nina. Seeing you with Derek makes me want, what I never can have. Isn't that what we crave most?" He put out his hand. "Let's call it a truce, shall we?"

Nina took his hand tentatively. Moving back, he nodded towards a blue and white houseboat which was tethered close at hand. Paradise Revisited was the name of the houseboat. He leapt aboard, and in a moment, they lowered a log over which Nina walked across. She was surprised by the elegant interiors. All pale green and beige. The houseboat had an entire suite of rooms with an awning at the side, where one could sit and watch the passing scenes, as the boat glided through the water. Nina was so entranced that she did not know when Roy left, and Derek bounded into the boat.

There were three men on board, two oarsmen and the cook. The boat was motorised but had a canoe, locally called 'vanji', tied to the sides. Tourists were taken in the vanji, through narrow canals, into islands redundant with wildlife. Derek had specially requested to be taken to an island. They would be visiting Padiramanal, an island, less popular than the well-known tourist attraction, Kumaragan, which thronged with visitors all year long.

Padiramanal, mused Nina, as she stretched out on the long seat under the awning, was a name evocative of something mysterious. She was replete with food that included a variety of dishes, some familiar and others newly discovered. She had liked the beetroot pacchadi and asked for a second helping. It was a yoghurt-based dish, and Nina was quick to swallow a couple of enzymes. She was lactose intolerant, but an occasional overindulgence was forgiven with the help of a lactose enzyme supplement.

The boat had halted at the very edge of a mangrove. Through half-shut eyes, Nina viewed the reflection of the silver water as it played across her face. If she turned her eyes towards the mangrove, she could see the dragonflies, their wings gossamer in the half-light. The boat bobbed gently, lulling her already surfeited senses. It was so serene. Heavenly, Nina thought as she grew drowsy, a state of stupor between wakefulness and sleep. She was drifting, falling, when she jerked awake. There was something cold and clammy against her stomach, slowly edging its way lower and onto her side. A reptile, perhaps out of the mangrove was her first thought. Then, she felt fingers rip apart the waistband of her jeans. She clamped down on a wriggling forehand. The hand wrestled with her own and to her surprise suddenly withdrew. Her sides were smarting, and she could see a smudge of blood against the seams of the jeans. Sitting up, she caught sight of two figures, one in pursuit of the other. One of the oarsmen had jumped off the boat and must have dragged the attacker off her. Nina knew without a doubt that the caduceus had provoked the attack. She sat up, her insides churning as she retched; dry, gasping retches which hurt her throat. Instinctively, she reached for the caduceus which she wore slung low, over her hip. It had gone. Overwhelmed with horror, Nina screamed.

Derek was sitting at the open bow of the boat, just a foot away from the overhanging branches, on which he had discovered a heron rookery. To his delight, some chicks were just launching out of their nest. The boat passing so close to the heron's nests had roused cries of alarm, which stilled as the boat docked. Camera in hand, Derek waited for the spectacle of a baby bird's first winged venture into the green, lush world of plants and water. A flicker of a movement caught his eye. One of the oarsmen was diving into the water. Roy. Derek had recognised him despite his disguise: the cloth wound around the head and a heavy beard. Derek had noticed how Roy pirouetted on his heels when in a hurry. No two people had the same gait. Roy's gait was as distinctive as his fingerprint would be. Derek had put his presence down to his obvious obsession with Nina. He was stalking her. But, now was not the time to call him out. Derek leaned over to see Roy tug at and swim alongside someone, who seemed to be fighting to get away. The second figure was much smaller. Just as he managed to train his binoculars on them, he heard Nina scream.

Nina was sitting in a crouched position examining the cut along her hip bone. It was shallow and had stopped bleeding. The cook and the oarsman wanted to turn around and make for the nearest police station. Derek stopped them with a shake of his head and asked them to bring Nina some coffee with plenty of sugar.

Back in their cabin, Derek produced a small charm which he had found as he knelt to help Nina up from the seat. It must have fallen during Nina's struggle to escape the assault. Nina gasped as she recognised it. A tiny, gold snake with emeralds for eyes and a forked tongue. She had seen it dangling from a chain on Maya chechi's wrist. As her eyes met Derek's, she knew he had noticed it too.

"Maya chechi?"

Derek nodded. He pulled down Nina's waistband and cleaned out the cut before applying an antiseptic.

The door opened sharply on its hinges, and Roy entered, water dripping from his clothes. He stared at Nina, his agitation making the vein on his forehead stand up.

"Are you hurt?"

Wordlessly, Nina held out the charm, her eyes questioning.

Roy sat down on his haunches.

Taking the charm from Nina, he said, "Amma's."

"But, why Roy? Why?"

"For me. Wait, let me explain," said Roy. "The caduceus is a family heirloom. It was always handed over to the eldest daughter of the family. Shanti chechi was given it by her mother, and later, she gave it to you."

"Did Maya chechi ever want it?"

"She never coveted it until recently... until she knew its true worth. Not as a mere ornament, but something which wields power."

"Even so. And here I was thinking she really cared for me."

"She does care for you. Still does."

"And yet?" asked Nina her eyes moist with pain and anger.

Roy looked away. His jaws were clenched, and the room fell silent.

"It's hard to explain human motives. Way too complex. Amma always resented being the poor relative. Shanti chechi would come with her parents to Kodungallur on her summer vacations. There would be gifts galore for everyone and of course some hand-me-downs. Shanti chechi's toys, story books, frocks… things she had outgrown or grown bored with. Ironically, the pattern extended into their adult lives," he paused.

"They hardly meet and when they do, they seem to have so much to share," said Nina.

Roy continued as if Nina had not spoken.

"My dad wanted to marry Shanti chechi who turned down the proposal. My mother was the second choice. That rankled."

"My mother never mentioned any of this." Nina was startled by the disclosure.

"But what has all this to do with her attempt to wrest the caduceus away?" asked Derek curtly.

Roy's glance flickered to him and back to Nina.

"Amma never thought about the caduceus or of stealing it. Not until its true power was known. The diaries and her casual conversations with Prof. Shankara Menon made her realise that the caduceus is both an amulet and a magic wand. She realised that it would open up trade over the high seas. We have many business ventures which require us to have secure passage across the sea. With piracy reaching the proportions it has, possessing the caduceus would have been of enormous benefit."

"What about you Roy?" asked Derek. "Were you in this with her? On the day Nina saw someone at the window, you were out there. Someone saw the caduceus on the floor and knew Nina wore it around her waist. Your clothes were mud-stained."

"It was neither me nor my mother. It was a man who had come in out of the rain. I saw him and thought him a weary wayfarer taking shelter in the rain. It was only when he prised open your window and peered in, that I moved forward to accost him. He vaulted over the wall of the veranda, and I followed. The rain swallowed him up, and I returned to my room. That's when I heard a sound. Didn't realise it was you. Thought it was the intruder again and came down to investigate. I did not want to raise an alarm because Amma was already upset about intruders on our property."

"She is a strong woman to have swum across and attempted to steal the caduceus," said Derek. "How did she manage to swim and grapple for the prize?" Derek was intrigued. His anger had evaporated. Roy was a better man than he imagined him to be. The confession could not have been easy.

"Maya chechi was always someone, I gravitated towards while growing up. There were things, I found easier to tell her because she would not grow overtly anxious like my mother. This is most unexpected.

Roy, I would rather have lost the caduceus than have learned that Maya chechi planned and plotted to take it away from me. So, now what?"

Roy was silent. And then drawing himself onto his feet, he said "To her, it was not theft." He paused. "She was merely taking what she thought belonged to her, by right. I stopped her, Nina, and we will no more trouble you. More importantly, there is someone else out there, who wants it as desperately as amma did. I won't make excuses for her actions. This has torn it, hasn't it? Nina?"

Nina didn't answer. She was wondering about the caduceus. Did Maya chechi have it? Had it sunk to the bottom, slipping out of her hand during the scuffle? She was just about to ask Roy when she remembered. She had placed it in the hollow of her cosmetic case among the make-up sponges.

She said, "It's hard, Roy, to reconcile… to accept that Maya chechi would have no scruples in taking something away that belonged to another. And to think she could break all bonds of affection and act only in self-interest. It's goodbye, Roy."

She walked to Roy and gave him a hug. Roy held her tight, and then after a wave to Derek, leapt to the ground and raced out of sight.

Chapter XIII

To be, or not to be: That is the Question:

Nina led Derek to Sarah Cohen's shop. Her mother wanted some laces to sew onto the bottom of her petticoats. Her mother, Nina knew, was a stickler for details when it came to living life aesthetically. There was always a fresh flower arrangement, gracing the living room, made from the flowers and herbs which grew in the garden. She put together everything from periwinkles to curry leaves to make the most eye-catching of arrangements. Had she called Maya chechi, Nina wondered. Her mother would never forgive Maya chechi for the betrayal. Nor, thought Nina could she. Hurt and bewilderment were replaced by fury. Nina was infuriated not because Maya chechi had coveted the caduceus or been devious; that, of course, had come as a surprise. It was the utter callousness that Maya chechi had displayed that revolted her.

Derek interrupted her with, "Here you are. Looks like the only thriving shop in this ghost town."

"Her legacy continues," said the man behind the counter in impeccable English.

Nina remembered the lady with her soft, white hair and gentle demeanour from her earlier visits with her mother. Sarah Cohen was a Pardeshi Jew, who had stayed on when most of the others migrated to Israel and other parts of the world. Nina was fascinated by the intricately woven, exquisite doilies of lace and bought a few she could frame and display, on the wooden panelling of her office.

Stepping out of the darkened interiors into the brilliant sunshine, she did not see the young, albino boy till he spoke to her. Derek's hand on her elbow tightened.

"Tour of the Jew town, madam?"

"No, thanks." Nina put on her sunglasses and moved away.

"The synagogue?" the boy persisted. "Madam, the last prayer service for the day starts in fifteen minutes. A rabbi from Israel… You must come."

The boy's tone had turned insistent, and his pale blue eyes, with their white lashes had widened in an appeal.

Was there more to the request than was apparent? Nina was confused. They had planned on going to the synagogue, anyway. Nina stopped and turned to Derek. He nodded, and they followed the boy's darting figure through the narrow, winding streets.

Nina was enchanted, as always, by the ornate interiors of the synagogue. The Belgian glass chandeliers shone brightly as if they had just been polished. Some of them hung askew because the chains holding them had grown warped with time. The light falling through the stained glass windows made kaleidoscopic designs on the floor. On the Tebah, the elevated platform used to read scrolls and perform religious services, a man stood wearing priestly robes. The service had just finished, and the prayer chamber was empty, except for the figure that crouched in the corner. At their entry, the priest turned around. He slowly descended from the platform, making his way towards them. He was looking at Nina, and his deep, blue eyes blazed with recognition. She knew him from Nice, and she had seen him run past to rescue her when she was being pursued along the Kukkarahalli Lake. It was probably the same man who had boarded the flight with her. There was a connection; they could not be random thoughts. Nina stifled a scream. Instinct told her to run, but Derek stood, his body supporting her, his arm enveloping her in a half hug.

"I am Nicholas. Do not be afraid of me. I am a very distant cousin or uncle. We will figure it out. We can both claim Nani Kutty's mother as our ancestor."

Nina slumped with relief. She took the proffered hand and felt her own held in a strong grip.

"And you must be Derek," Nicholas said turning to shake hands with Derek.

"It is a long story, no more curious than many which have been told in the sanctum of this synagogue."

Nicholas spoke of their meeting with his parents at Shimla. The Israeli couple had been struck by

Nina's resemblance to an ancestor in a painting that graced their home. The man in the painting was a Pardeshi Jew as many of their relations had been. His grandmother had married a German which accounted for Nicholas's blond looks. His mother, Nicholas said, had recognised the caduceus Nina wore around her neck; the medallion on a chain. It was the replica of the caduceus on a ring which their family treasured as a legacy. Nicholas displayed it. Smaller than the medallion, it had the same insignia studded with sparkling jewels.

Nina told him about what she had learned from the two personal documents which they had unearthed. The picture that hung in their home must have been that of Nani Kutty's twin brother. The mother, Radha, must have tied the caduceus to him. Had she been conscious when the child was given away? Would she have wanted to identify the child at a later date, or was it to give him his father's legacy? These were questions which could never be answered, smothered, as they were, by the weight of time. Nevertheless, they haunted Nina. Nicholas had no answers to these questions. He knew only about the events, which had brought Nina to the Jew town of Mattancherry.

The caduceus, or the sighting of it in Nina's possession, had set off an alarm. Nicholas was a seafarer, who knew that it was an insignia both revered and sought after. It could ensure a smooth passage through the seas. Those who led their lives on the sea lived by rules far removed from the International

Treaties on maritime trade. These bound only a few. The caduceus bound the others. Once, it was the possession of a few regular seafarers from Greece on whom it had been bestowed for being loyal in their service to the king and their country. The caduceus was a prized possession, a recognition of the services rendered. It was a badge of honour to possess a caduceus. It also gained fame and acceptance among those whose lives were a series of notorious exploits. Thus, it was that the caduceus came to be coveted by the righteous and thieves alike. What Nina wore, as a mere ornament, had power so potent that it could rescue humans from penury and raise them to citadels of power. It could, in the long run, even change the destiny of nations.

"So", asked Nina, "you think it is wasted on me?"

"When no one knew about it, owning a caduceus did not matter. Now, it does, Nina. I came to ensure it was not stolen from you. You could have been harmed…"

"Was it you then? That time at the Kukkarahalli Lake?"

"YES, and many times in Europe. Danger followed at your heels and so did I." Nicholas grinned wryly. "You could have been assaulted more than once."

"I saw recognition in the eyes of total strangers. But that was not me they saw. It was the caduceus. Some seemed to want to warn me. The man you pushed into the lake? Would he have attempted to overwhelm me for the caduceus?"

"He would not have. He was an ally though I didn't know it when I fell, pummelling him, into the lake."

"Ally?" asked Derek. He was looking at the figure approaching them. It was the man who had been kneeling, deep in prayer. The gait was distinct. Derek froze, his hands going to his pocket. Nicholas glanced at him, but he made no move

"Roy?" Nina mouthed. "What are you here for?"

Drawing close to Derek, she glanced from Nicholas to Roy and back, her eyes questioning.

It was Nicholas who answered. "We were strangers, Nina, till you brought us together. Roy had heard through the grapevine, which is efficient on land and sea, that a caduceus had surfaced in Mysore. He came to buy it. It is indeed, invaluable for a trader whose ships ply the seas. When he found that it was you who possessed it, he began to shadow you. Not to rob you of it, but to guard you."

"Nina, you were jaywalking across a landmine," interrupted Roy, "totally unaware of the consequences. Did you notice, that I boarded the same flight as you? And the scarf, you wore around your neck, read like an invitation. No one needed to look among your baggage for the caduceus."

Nicholas said, "He was an ally, in my effort, to keep you and the caduceus safe. You are one of us, Nina. The caduceus is yours. And by right, it should belong to you. I just need you to know that it is no mere ornament. You can no longer wear it with elan. Its true purpose is to help traders over the sea."

"There is a lot of legit trade which happens with absolutely no intervention, except the requisite license. Captain Hook is the stuff of faded, fairy tales. Piracy has not disappeared, and an increase in piracy activities has been reported in recent years. So, I can see the rationale which brought you, both, here." said Derek.

"What would a land animal know about the adventures at sea?" challenged Roy.

"Much more than you would expect. And not merely from reading Peter Pan or Moby Dick," quipped Derek.

Roy continued to look at him with raised eyebrows. Derek turned to Nicholas and said, "What I do know is that despite a ban on the harvesting of bullfrogs since the mid-nineteen eighties, their export as gourmet fare continues, causing them to dwindle at a rate which threatens extinction. Illegal tiger farms, all over the world, carry on trade over the sea. Perhaps, possessing a caduceus helps abet such unlawful trade."

He paused and turning to Roy, he added, "That would concern a conservationist. All animals, those on land or at sea deserve to live and multiply unmolested."

"You could not have explained our predicament better," intervened Nicholas. "The caduceus, should not fall into the wrong hands, Derek.

Turning and holding his hands out in an appeal, Nicholas continued,

"Nina, I followed you to India. Of course, I had for long contemplated visiting Mattancherry to pay homage to the land of my forefathers. I also had to meet you to get to the bottom of the mystery… your uncanny resemblance to a portrait of my ancestor and the caduceus in your keeping. My meeting with Roy was an act of serendipity though he may not quite agree. I would not have left India without attempting to meet you. I was planning on getting Roy to set up a meeting. We are related, Nina, and there is so much to catch up on. Derek and Nina, come stay with us in our Kibbutz. My parents will be all too happy."

Nina smiled her thanks at Nicholas. "But we have not settled the issue of how to keep the caduceus safe, or who keeps it?"

"Name your sum and I will pay. The caduceus will serve me well."

"I don't know if I can match his bid," said Roy. "But I need it to ensure that our overseas trade happens without a hitch. With the caduceus, we can ensure a smooth passage. I will make you a full partner, Nina. Half the profit is yours."

Nina looked from Roy to Nick and back again. Their visages blended and blurred. Was Roy towing his mother away when she was being attacked, or was he helping to keep her afloat till the task was accomplished? And, how much did she know of Nick? Could Nanikutty's twin be his ancestor? She would never know. Let the dead past bury its dead. She could not remember who had said that to her. Maya chechi, perhaps?

"The caduceus is not for sale. Not now, not ever. It was a token of love, and a symbol of my marriage. I may have to deposit it in a vault. So be it, but it stays with me."

Nicholas took a step forward, his eyes beseeching. Roy turned away. The door of the synagogue creaked open as four people entered. They all wore rifles across their shoulders.

"My team from Idduki," smiled Derek pleasantly.

"Elephant menace on the road leading to the Cochin airport. But we were able to get the rogue elephant with a tranquillizer gun. Thank God, there was no need for these," said the man in the lead pointing to his rifle.

"And now for the airport," said Derek.

Their receding footsteps sounded like an army marching through the strangely silent sanctuary. They left behind two figures, standing, as if frozen in time.

Chapter XIV

Rescue Comes, but Freedom?

Derek had come at the request of the Voice for Asian Elephants Society to Trivandrum. The VFAES, in partnership with the Kerala Forest Department, planned to restore and expand the Nilambur corridor to facilitate the movement of elephants. This would prevent the frequent conflict between plantation owners and elephants. Derek believed that there were no 'crop raiders' or 'rampaging rogue elephants'. The rampant encroachment of humans had cut off the spaces, that elephants had been using for decades, to move to forests and sanctuaries. This situation created a conflict between vested human interests and the need of elephants to move unhindered. The project, Derek was overseeing, required close coordination as it moved through the various phases, leading ultimately to the knitting together of elephant corridors across the country. This would prevent inbreeding among the elephants and ensure their survival. Derek, along with representatives of several NGOs and government organisations across the country, had arrived at a blueprint of the plan. The Supreme Court had also ruled in their favour and ordered the closure of resorts, which had sprouted like mushrooms, narrowing the elephant corridors. That was something to celebrate, but there was so much yet to do. But Derek found himself unable to focus on the work at hand. He had become uneasy about the long drawn out silence behind which Nina had retreated. Their conversations over the phone sounded stilted when he played it back in his mind. Nina was not really talking; she was merely mouthing formalities. She was also not persuading him to come. Something was going on, and Derek knew he had to go and discover what it was. That is how he arrived unannounced, dripping wet at the doorstep like a drowned sailor.

As he climbed in beside the driver of the open jeep, in which his team members had arrived along with the staff from Kerala Forest Department, he knew it could all have ended differently. The entry of the armed team had changed the game in their favour. It was sheer good luck; nothing had been planned. An elephant on a rampage had brought them to the highway near Mattancherry. His message, asking to be picked up from the synagogue where he knew their exploration would end, had brought the crew at the very moment, when some kind of a confrontation seemed inevitable. Something told him that the game was not over yet.

They lowered the foldable steps leading into the jeep. As Nina ascended, she felt a sudden spasm in her underbelly which made her gasp aloud. One of the men in the team reached down to help her climb in. The jungle safari jeep had seats all along the sides. Nina sat down on the nearest; she felt another spasm tearing her insides. The man who had helped her bent solicitously and asked whether she was in pain. When she nodded, he opened his backpack and handed her a muscle relaxant. She drank it down with several gulps of water as thirst surged through her. The jeep had begun to move through the old town. Nina could see a few people, tourists mainly, staring at the unusual spectacle of a woman surrounded by gun-toting men. Perhaps, they thought she was being taken hostage. Is this what adrenaline did? Her mind was working in total dissonance with her body. Nina recognised the absurdity of the situation even as she felt something slide down into her panty, followed by a spurt of wetness. She instinctively knew that she was having a spontaneous abortion. There was nothing to be done except to accept the inevitable. She felt numbed. This could not be happening. Tying a jacket around her waist, she asked to speak to Derek. The man, who must have been asked to attend to her, handed over his microphone. After a few crackling sounds, Derek called out her name. She quickly explained why they needed to stop. The blood had begun to trickle down and stain the insides of her trousers. The man, in attendance, gave her a startled glance before taking the phone from her. He barked out a few instructions to the driver and stood with his back turned to her. He was like a wall, shielding her from the sight of the others in the jeep. The other men stood looking away. They seemed impervious and yet, when the jeep came to a halt, they acted in unison to lift her gently into the wheelchair outside the hospital. At the emergency, the gynaecologist took her vitals. Yes, there were foetal remains with the bloody discharge. An injection would stop the excess bleeding. It would be like a normal menstrual flow. She could take the flight as planned.

Nina changed her clothes. Grief and rage tore through her as she clawed at the chain, with the medallion, around her neck. She felt trapped, the chain a noose. For a moment, she was tempted to dump it, along with her soiled clothes, in the garbage bin. But, something held her back. It had been her companion for long, and she had uncovered so much of the history which was connected with the medallion. It was no more a prize to be fought for. It was for Nina, an inheritance worth preserving. There was no time to grieve, she had to press on towards the finish. She would not surrender. Not yet, not ever.

Outside the ward, Derek stood awaiting her. He held her in his arms and stroked her head. She had seen him soothe frightened animals, in a shelter, just so. She shuddered with effort as she swallowed a laugh rising in her throat. Then Derek said, "Nina, we have a long time to ensure that the caduceus is passed on to our children. As many as you want… a large house, and a garden, echoing with the sound of their laughter."

Nina found that she could walk to the jeep. The darkness, which had shrouded her, lifted. Derek's words were like a sliver of light which illuminated the path ahead. There would be days when she would grieve her loss, but life held anew the promise of adventure, of exploring unknown terrains. Life beckoned, and she would go where it took her.

There was another safari jeep in place of the earlier one. That team had left to take care of an emergency, in the town of Cochin, created by an adolescent, bull elephant. Derek explained that a young, male elephant, like a teenager, was a cocktail of hormones. With high levels of testosterone running through their veins, young bull elephants entered a state referred to as 'musth'. This was a state in which, frenzied by their intense need to mate, they would swagger around making trouble. In this state, they were very aggressive and a threat to both wildlife and humans alike. With a strong-smelling fluid running down their temples, from the temporal glands, and a constant dribble of urine through their sheathed penises, they advertised their blatant masculinity and the need to copulate. This, surge of testosterone, had led a young bull elephant to terrorise Kochi for several hours.

The young bull had entered one of the busiest areas in Kochi at dawn. He had killed a petty shop owner, just as the man was downing his shutter, before entering the parking lot of a Mall. When the guards discovered him, the elephant was walking up a ramp. The circus, soon, drew quite a few spectators who began to shout and clap. Then, the mob, set off firecrackers to chase him away, but unfortunately, they let loose a furious, maddened creature upon the city. The elephant chased buses and autos along the city's roads until it was captured by the Kerala Wildlife Rescue team.

"Double rescue," muttered Nina. "First us and then them."

Leaning back against Derek's shoulder, Nina shut her eyes. The medicines were having a soporific effect, and she drifted off to sleep. She was suddenly awoken by the jeep jolting to a halt.

The driver turned to Derek. "Sir, roadblock."

"Roadblock?" queried Derek.

"Strike sir. Not unusual in Kerala."

Derek asked, "How far are we from the airport?"

"Less than an hour."

The team leader, who was sitting next to the driver, was speaking on his mobile.

He turned to Derek and said, "We can try to muscle past but you will miss your flight."

"What is the problem?" asked Derek.

"We have information, from my men sent to mingle with the strikers, that this may be a sham protest. There are locals, paid to participate and swell the core group of protesters, blocking the road, but the majority are not familiar with the local language. They communicate in a language our men do not understand. But they are waiting."

"For what? whom?" asked Nina.

Derek was silent. After a long pause, Derek asked, "For US?"

"Perhaps," was the answer.

"Would an ambulance get us through?" asked Nina.

"An ambulance will be immediately suspected. And we don't want to use pellet guns to disperse the crowds. Or to shoot. Too many questions to answer later. This is a seemingly peaceful protest. But someone in the crowd may manage to swarm up, into the vehicle, defying the armed guards."

Looking at Nina, he asked, "Will you be able to climb a ladder? I can call a helicopter."

"Gopinath," said Derek, addressing the man, "where will you get one? The protesters seem to be heading this way."

They could hear the faint bang and crash of music, the noise of a clamorous crowd approaching.

"We have a rescue helicopter on standby since the bull calf was rampaging through Kochi. Fortunately, our men have succeeded in tranquilising it. I have already asked them to come. I can see no other way out. You will be taken straight to the Lalith Mahal Helipad, where the Karnataka Forest Department officials will receive and escort you."

The rest of what he spoke was drowned in the whooping sound of a chopper approaching. As it hovered in the air over them, above the din of the chopper blades came the deafening sound of drums and cymbals. The procession had reached them.

"This one we missed," muttered Gopinath. He swung swiftly into the back of the jeep, barking some instructions into his phone. Their armed escorts jumped onto the ground and stood, rifles held in readiness. Meanwhile, a long ladder was let down from the chopper. Nina held it with hands that were moist. Gingerly, she put a foot on the first rung. The noise of the singing and music made her go dizzy with fear. As adrenaline swept through her body, she climbed up, Derek close behind her. From her seat, she looked down transfixed. The group of religious revellers were celebrating the birth of Lord Krishna. There were local people and lighter-skinned ones of foreign origin among them. Some men were tonsured and in ochre robes. Brought to a halt by the presence of the armed guards, they looked up. Among the blur of faces, Nina wondered if there were any she could recognise. With a sigh, she leaned back to gaze at the panoramic view of the sea and sky through which they were travelling. They had escaped. As relief swept over, her, her eyes fell on the medallion with the caduceus. It had fallen out of her shirt, and in the clear light of the sky, it glittered wickedly.